From the diary of Winston Weyn, camper, former Cabin Leader and Chief of Propaganda in the revolution at High Pines:

June 6

I am not going to write much because I am very tired. I am also scared and I suppose I am still excited....Today a Supreme Revolutionary Committee was formed, but I'm not a member. Everyone on the Supreme Revolutionary Committee has to be at least a captain. Frank and Stanley are generals, of course, and Frank had me announce all their names and ranks on the public address system. And that is about all that happened all day except for one terrible thing. Frank Divordich of all people got tired of the revolution and said the cooking was lousy and just started to walk right out of camp. But he was stopped by a guard and taken to Colonel Blackridge and he took Divordich up to the meadow and tied him to a tree and actually beat Divordich on the back with a belt. Hard! Poor Divordich was plenty mad when he came back to the cabin and he wouldn't even tell anyone what happened but late last night he told me about it because he was crying and I heard him. I saw his back and it has got big marks on it all right. He says it still hurts and I'm both mad and scared about this. Frank said no one was going to get hurt. It is time we stopped this whole thing....

The Butterfly Revolution

William Butler

BALLANTINE BOOKS • NEW YORK

A Ballantine Book
Published by The Random House Publishing Group

Copyright © 1961 by William Butler

Published in the United States by Ballantine Books, an imprint of The Random House Publishing Group, a division of Random House, Inc., New York.

Ballantine and colophon are registered trademarks of Random House, Inc.

Library of Congress Catalog Card Number: 67-10948

www.ballantinebooks.com

ISBN 0-345-33182-6

This edition published by arrangement
with G.P. Putnam's Sons

OPM   47   46   45   44   43   42   41

First Ballantine Books Edition: December 1967
Thirtieth Printing: December 1993

Cover Art by Bruce Pennington

To Dr. Harold Winkler

The Butterfly Revolution

MAY 25

My thirteenth birthday, and this diary from my Uncle Giles. My name, Winston Weyn, embossed on it in gold. I have never seen such a big diary. I guess it would be very heavy if the pages weren't so thin. Uncle Giles told me I will be very pleased with myself if I keep up with my diary, and he said he will get me another one next year if I do.

Uncle Giles also gave me a copy of *Bleak House* by Charles Dickens, because a few months ago I told him I enjoyed *David Copperfield*, but I have already read a little bit of *Bleak House* and it doesn't seem much good to me, it looks a little weepy. I really do like Uncle Giles but nothing makes me madder than getting presents I don't appreciate. Anyhow, I'm reading Herodotus now, which is extremely interesting, so I'll just have to put *Bleak House* away in my bookcase.

This whole day stunk, mostly. No one would ever have known it was my birthday. The worst thing about the day was the present my parents gave me, which is a trip to one of those cheap city-run summer camps. I know kids who go to these camps, and the only things they do there are run around and yell and play baseball and swim. I am too skinny to swim. I think my father gave me this trip because he thinks it would be nice if I were like other kids. I'm supposed to spend a month up there somewhere, by a river above Wellberg, with a bunch of kids who are always running or wrestling or screaming or giggling at dirty words. I wish I knew why my father wants me to be like other kids.

I will have to write a little smaller. I am running out of space. Anyhow, I'm sitting in bed and I hear my mother coming, which means she is coming with the Bible, which means it is time for our nightly chapter. We have read the whole Bible once and now we're reading it again, and we are back in the Pentateuch. She doesn't understand any of it but she always tries to explain the violent parts, like they are dirty windows which maybe she can hide with lacy words. Well, I am an atheist and have been for a whole year now, nearly.

This is not enough space, because I write very fast and would like to write more, but the page ends here.

MAY 26

Just one more day of school. I found out today that Pete Bunch and Eddy Hoag are going to High Pincs, the same summer camp I am going to, and they are going on the same day. If I had any interest in going at all, that sure would have killed it. Pete Bunch is fourteen and is a year behind. He likes to walk around in his gym shorts, strutting empty-chested and empty-headed down by the girls' volleyball courts.

Speaking of Eddy Hoag, today, after school, Eddy and Norman Poole were out behind the girls' gym, and I was surprised to see them holding Marge Pinelli and Dorothy Wills up to the wire fence there, necking and feeling around and stuff. Norman saw me and he said, "You want Marge for a while?" I just answered, "No." The girls laughed and Dorothy Wills said, "I'm glad there's at least *one* good boy around here," like every other guy in the school except me had been feeling her or something. The thing is, those girls were enjoying themselves, and so I felt kind of creepy to refuse Norman's invitation and just walk away. Somehow I thought I should have felt at least one of them just for the appearance of things.

Now I better begin to hide this diary, because if my mother finds it, boy, she will keep me in Job until Christmas.

MAY 27

This was the last day of school for this term. It was only half a day, actually, but that was all I needed to get in a screwy argument with a couple of kids.

Sandy Person said that girls do not belch, so we argued about it, and my good friend, Pete Bunch, comes up and says, "Hell, don't argue with Winnie Weyn, man. *She* ought to *know*." So Sandy said, "That's right, I never *did* hear Winnie belch. Belch, Winnie!" And then some kids tried to get me to belch and just wouldn't let me alone, so I had to go away. People can sure be cruel. It isn't as though I went around doing things to make people cruel, either. Pete is the guy who started to call me "Winnie" and so a lot of guys do it now. I am certainly sorry that guy is going to High Pines.

My mother is always saying, "It is the little things that count," and generally I don't put much stock in what my mother says, but I noticed in Herodotus today that Darius became king because his horse neighed, which is a pretty little thing, taken by itself. So I am thinking more and more about how little things make big things happen.

Well, there is more space, but I have no more to write today.

MAY 28

I think it would be better not to have the pages dated, as they are, so I can just write however much or little I have to write. And so I am crossing out all the dates in this book, and then I won't have to crowd my writing or leave blank spaces, either one. Question: will the diary last more than a year or less than a year that way?

This morning, after breakfast, I went to my room to read Herodotus. I was reading for about half an hour when Howard came in and said, "Hey, I hear you're going to camp with Pete Bunch."

I said, "Yes."

"Taking your books?" he asked, kind of sneering.

I don't understand why people who don't like books hate people who do like books, but there it is. Howard just happens to have one thing in common with Pete Bunch: they both admire ignorance. Howard is one year older, fifteen, and isn't a year behind like Pete, but his grades aren't very good, and sometimes I help him with his homework. In fact, I guess this is why he lets me live. Of course, Howard wants to go to college and so he tries to keep his work up, because after all he needs college experience if he's going to be a professional football player, like he wants to.

Well, anyhow, I had actually been thinking about taking some books to summer camp, because I certainly am going to have to do something while other kids are choosing pitchers and going swimming. So, to Howard, I said, "Maybe."

"Nope," Howard said quite positively, "you aren't."

"Why not?"

"Because I'm going to camp too, that's why not, and I'm not having my brother drag along a pile of books. You just better understand that."

I asked him how it was he was going, since it was my birthday present. He said he was going and he knew about it long before I did, but no one said anything because it was going to be a surprise for my birthday.

I said, "Thanks."

He picked up his fist and let me look at it. "You bring along even one book and I'm going to dump both you and it in the river and make sure neither one comes up. You hear?"

"I won't go, then."

"That's up to you," and he shrugged and sort of groped out of my room like a big anthropomorphized yawn.

It was maybe ten minutes later that my father came in to say, "What's this about you not going to camp?"

"Well, can I take some books?" I asked him.

"Why do you want to take books to camp?"

I didn't say anything, so my father got mad and said, "You're going to camp, Win, and I don't think you'll have to take any books with you. You'll have plenty to do up there. There won't be time for books."

I tried to argue about that, but my father interrupted me:

"You try to be different, Win. You *try* to be different. It's not healthy. Now, you're going to camp with

Howard, and you're going to do what the other boys do. You're going to be like other boys for a change. You hear? That's the end of it," and he kind of flicked himself out of the room like a big anthropomorphized bull-whip flicking itself in case someone had forgotten it was there.

That was the morning. I spent the rest of the day deciding to take some books anyhow.

MAY 29

To church, where the Reverend Munson chose the 20th chapter of Matthew, verses 1 to 16, which tell a story about how the Kingdom of Heaven is the same as a man who hires people to work in a vineyard; and how some work less and some work more, but they all get paid exactly the same amount.

Sometimes when I read the Bible it seems like Herodotus, and I enjoy it, but the way the Reverend Munson talks about it is the same as when Mr. Nido talks about Benjamin Franklin and Thomas Jefferson at school, which is very dull, so that the only thing which interested me is why the Kingdom of Heaven is like a place where some people might have to work as long as eleven hours every day. I also notice that the people got paid only a penny a day (whether they worked one hour or eleven hours), and I wonder that those people never went on strike. Of course, the Reverend Munson's idea was the generosity of Heaven, but it sounded to me like it would be best to get into Heaven last because there would be less work to do.

Well, in two days I leave for camp with Howard. I will have to wait till the last minute before putting my books in my bag. Howard says there are cabins at High Pines and about eight boys stay in each cabin, and the biggest boys stay in cabins way across the camp from the cabins where smaller boys stay. Am I a big boy or a small boy? I guess I won't know till I get to camp, but Howard seems cheerful, so I guess he thinks I'm a small boy.

Uncle Giles was here for lunch and while my father was out watering, he and Mama had one of those sudden rows. Sometimes Uncle Giles makes a joke about my father's work (my father works for the bill-collecting department in a loan company), or about religion, and this time it was something about interest rates. As usual, Mama got mad and told me to go away. I don't always understand Uncle Giles and don't know if his jokes are bad or not, but I try to understand him because he's a smart man and works for a newspaper. I don't know what the joke was today, and the only way I could tell it was a joke was that Uncle Giles laughed at it himself.

My bookcase is now getting full. There are only three shelves, of course, and all in all I guess I have about sixty-five books, so pretty soon I will have to have a new bookcase. I like to look at the bookcase. Books make me feel important, especially if I have read them, which is another reason I get peeved by having books I don't want to read. I figure that, if no one bothered me, I could read maybe twenty-five books before school begins again, maybe even more. It takes me longer to read long books, or books which are difficult, and Herodotus is both long and difficult, so I've been reading it slowly. Most of my books, though, have been just stories and quite easy. I still like to read Terhune, too, because I like collie dogs very much. I have read Burgess and *Winnie the Pooh* and *The House at Pooh Corner,* which were presents from Uncle Giles a long time ago, for an obvious reason. Lately, though, I have mostly liked books which are not just stories, like history books, and I have a little paperback about political philosophers which is something like my paperback on religions of the world, though more difficult, and I mean to read it soon. History is the most interesting of all and I can hardly believe some of what I have read in the Bible and in Herodotus, such as the story about Harpagus and the beast-king, Astyages, or the things I just don't understand yet, such as how all the women of this one town had to sleep with some strange man at least once in their lives, even the noble-women, and how men would come up to them where they waited at this temple and any man at all could flip a coin into the lap of any woman, and she had to go with him no matter who he was and sleep with him, so that she was being forced in this way to be a prostitute at least that one time in her life; and it told how some of the uglier women would wait at that temple maybe three or four years before a man would flip a coin at them. Herodotus says that all this was shameful, and I agree with him.

I hide my diary behind the bookcase now.

MAY 30

Reading over what I wrote yesterday, I would like to add this about books and knowledge: I feel that there is nothing that people cannot know, and therefore there is nothing that I cannot know. I don't know why, but believing this is very pleasant, I like the idea, and it is nice just to lie on my bed and think about that idea, just lie there and believe there is nothing I cannot know. And I really think it is exciting to know things.

For example, my paperback on religions taught me that religion has a lot to do with two things, namely, pain and death. So I began to think about these things and experimented by hurting myself, like pinching myself or pricking myself with a pin, and it seemed to me that pain was always the same as heat, and so I burned myself a little with a match, and boy, that hurt! But I found I could take it if I concentrated on the fire and my own skin, and then I learned that all these kinds of pain really were the same.

Well, I had a chance to test this in a more severe way, because one day I was taking a bath and my brother came in and used the toilet without any concern for me, which was disgusting of him, and I told him he might have waited. So he didn't even flush the toilet, which made me mad and I threw the soap at him from the bathtub and *crash!* it went right through the bathroom window. My father came running and stumbling into the bathroom and flicked me out of the bathtub and on through the house and out to the garage without stopping to inquire as to what had taken place, which is the usual kind of "trial" around here, and he took off his belt and began to give it to me hard right on my wet legs. I saw right off I had the chance to test my theory that pain doesn't exist unless you are afraid of it, so I began to concentrate hard as I could upon that belt and upon my legs and I thought right *into* each whack he gave me, and the only thing I felt was heat. Not only that, but it wasn't any worse than the pinching or pricking, and I felt so happy about proving my theory that I had to grin, and my father saw my grin and shouted:

"You're setting yourself against me!"

That was true, but it never did occur to me to set myself in favor of that strapping. He gave me a few extra twists of the belt for not applauding, I guess, and then sent me to my room.

In my room, I examined my legs and was really surprised to see I had red welts coming up on them, and so I pushed my head into my pillow and laughed and laughed to think that I had conquered that pain which always, up till then, made me hurt and cry so much.

What I believe is this: knowledge is pleasant and ignorance is pain, and that explains why I like my books so much.

I suggested to my father tonight that I didn't really care to go to camp, after all, and would as soon stay home, but he just told me I was going to have a swell time and I could tell from his tone that that is exactly what I am going to do.

Question: if I am no longer afraid of punishment,

why am I minding my father and going to camp when I'd rather not go? Well, I am still afraid of *him.* Maybe there is no way to stop being afraid of punishment.

MAY 31

I enjoy getting up before the sun comes up. There is something fresh and sweet about the very earliest part of the morning and this morning the sky was all shiny, almost a watery gray, and we had cold cereal for breakfast and then I got all ready and at the last minute put my books in my canvas bag, as I had planned, underneath my pajamas and undershirts and flashlight and stuff. The way things turned out, I didn't have to be sneaky, because Mama made a point at breakfast about me being sure to take the Bible.

I said, "I'm not supposed to take any books."

"Well," said my father, "your mother wants you to take your Bible, so go ahead."

Then, above Howard's moaning, my father said I could take along one or two other books, too, so long as I didn't take a whole big pile of them. I guess he thought I had planned to move my whole bookcase to High Pines. So I took my diary, Herodotus, my paperback about political philosophers and my dictionary.

And here I am, sitting on a thin and kind of smelly narrow mattress on my bunk in a cabin at High Pines. There are two other guys on their bunks, one writing and one of them, Bob McCarthy, is looking through my Bible. It is early but the lights go out at ten o'clock and anyhow I'd rather get my writing done before too many guys are in here jabbering.

So far it isn't so bad here. The ride in took about four hours, and that old bus was pretty slow a lot of the way. I was sitting next to a kid named Paul Indian (which is a fine name, although he says he is not even part Indian), and he's a nice guy. He's in the cabin next to this one. Some of the kids aren't so bad, but they aren't interested in the things that interest me.

Tonight, for example, right in this cabin, after dinner, there was a terrible farting contest. Three kids were having the contest to see who could do it the loudest, and before it was over no one was even in the cabin except the winner, Frank Divordich (spelling?), who for some reason felt pretty good about winning, but a few of us felt pretty bad.

Paul Indian is my age, thirteen, a couple of months older, and is intelligent. I was telling him some of the things I was reading in Herodotus and he told me some things about music. He has been taking piano lessons for almost five years and is learning to play a sonata by Beethoven.

Once we got to camp, we were all lined up and introduced to Mr. Warren, Director of High Pines, who gave us a talk about fair play and good health and camp rules, such as no swearing, no smoking, lights out at ten and things like that. Then we were introduced to the camp counselors, four men, or older guys anyhow, being maybe nineteen or even twenty. A guy named Edward Heinz is in charge of my group. He wears glasses and looks smart. My group is made up of kids of twelve and thirteen, so I'm not little and I'm not big, I'm in the middle.

We were told that each cabin was going to elect a Cabin Leader who has to see that camp rules are obeyed (about which I will write more in a minute). The guys in my cabin are all thirteen, I think, except maybe two, who are probably twelve. The guys are Willy Schunn, Bob Daly, Bob McCarthy, Fred Elston, Frank Divordich, Ezra Finley and Ham Pumpernil (who says his nickname of "Ham" was given to him because he has built crystal radio sets and is now building a short-wave station where he lives, but the guys have decided it is probably because his last name sounds like a kind of bread that he is called "Ham," and so some guys call him Ham Sandwich).

After putting our things away in our cabin, we went to the mess hall to have lunch, which was pretty good: stew, bread, plenty of Kool-aid to drink, grape flavor.

After lunch we had to go swimming. Since I couldn't swim, I said I didn't want to, but Ham Pumpernil was there to say he would teach me. I said I didn't have any swimming trunks. "Neither have I," he told me, "you don't even need them here. There are no girls around." So I couldn't get out of it and pretty soon there I was with the other kids, down at the shallow part of the river down the hill from our cabin, and Ham was teaching me to kick. After a while of this I was actually able to swim a little, although I wasn't daring to go into the deeper water (which was a little embarrassing, since kids much smaller than me were gliding around down there). Ham left me to take a swim in the deeper part, too, so I just went on lying on my stomach and kicking up shallow water and busying myself in that way.

Well, while I was practicing in this fashion, a big kid who was stark naked came over to stand beside me for a time. This was Frank Reilley, who is kind of a strange guy, and anyone would say so who got stared at out of Frank's big, almost purple-looking eyes, which sort of look like moons on a night when there's going to be a storm. Frank Reilley also has a curious smile, because I get the feeling when he smiles that the smile is kind of a favor or something, that anyhow Frank Reilley thinks a smile is a pretty good idea at the moment. He just doesn't look as if he likes to smile. But anyhow, what I meant to say was he came over and stood beside me, and this was the first time I met him, and I didn't know what to do, because I didn't want to stop swimming and stare at him and I felt pretty silly splashing around like that, with someone hovering right over me.

Finally Frank Reilley said, "What are you doing?"

So I stopped swimming and looked up at him.

"You Howard Weyn's brother?" he asked.

I said I was.

"I figured you were. Do you know the word *Lepidoptera?*"

I was wondering if it was a riddle but I just said, "No."

"Well you should, if you're smart like your brother says you are," Frank Reilley said, kicking at the water and splashing some on me. "All the dumb jerks in my cabin, your brother included, think I'm nuts when I tell them butterflies have scales. I hate dumbheads to sit in judgment on me. Where's your dictionary? Your brother said you brought a dictionary."

I told him my dictionary was in my cabin.

"Go on and get it, will you?"

But I didn't want to just run around the camp naked, so I just kind of grimaced up at him.

"Aren't you going to get it?" he asked in a minute. I looked at him a while longer and he went on, "My name is Frank Reilley. Your brother says you're nuts. I figure that's because you're smart and he's an ass. Come on, get the book for me."

Well, there was nothing to do but get it, so I darted up the hill to my cabin and brought my dictionary down and Frank Reilley looked up the word at once, and sure enough, *Lepidoptera* turned out to be another way of saying butterfly and it said right in the dictionary that the word *Lepidoptera* comes from the Greek word for "scaly." So I told Frank he could borrow the dictionary, and then we watched the guys diving off the high rock over the deep part of the river, and then Frank Reilley went off without even saying goodbye.

It was Fred Elston who brought my dictionary back later, because Fred already knew Frank Reilley and a number of the big guys here before ever coming to High Pines, and so I got to talking about some of the bigger guys with Fred. Fred told me Frank Reilley is very smart and he didn't know what I even meant when I asked him why Frank was kind of strange, but he certainly seemed strange to me. But Fred told me that Frank is very brave and he can be dared most things and he'll do anything he is challenged to do, so long as whoever challenges him will try it, too, and someone dared him to kiss a pretty teacher once and Frank did it and got punished, but the guy who dared him to do it chickened out and wouldn't do it. And Fred told me this about Frank Reilley's father, that he was a Baptist pastor who got killed accidentally by a cop during a gun-fight in their neighborhood. If this is true, I guess I can't blame Frank Reilley for being a little strange. And even though he is very hairy and makes me nervous, I will say this for him, that he apparently doesn't mind a guy liking books.

After swimming, we got dressed and went to the mess hall and had Kool-aid and cookies and then we took a hike around the camp with Edward Heinz. I have to admit that High Pines is very beautiful, and it seems to be a pretty huge place. After the bus drives in, you go along a path for a couple of hundred feet or so until you come to the Administration Building and beyond that there is the first group of cabins where the big guys are, including my brother and Pete Bunch, and over to the left of that there is the place called the Quad, which is a big clearing for campfires and meetings and stuff. The Administration Building is bigger than two cabins and this is where Mr. Warren has his office and where the cooks and Mr. Warren sleep, and where the nurse has her office. A nurse! Boy, I was surprised to learn there is a nurse up here. It seems she sleeps over at the girls' camp, down the river, but comes over here a couple hours each day. And there I was running around naked, to say nothing of bigger guys like Frank Reilley.

Well, you go beyond the Quad and then down another path, and you come to the river—and right above it are the cabins where my group stays. I haven't yet seen the cabins for the smallest kids, but they are somewhere up toward the front, on the other side of the Administration Building.

I didn't realize how different the air would be here, but it is, it's so fresh it's nearly like drinking-water, and it's all full of a big deep sweet smell from the pines which are everywhere. There are also some eucalyptus trees and cypresses and acacia trees and poplars and oaks and so on, but more than anything there are just those high rusty pines making the ground so soft with their needles, and they smell wonderful.

On our hike, we followed the river down quite a distance and came upon a path and went up it into a large and pretty meadow with a lot of little yellow flowers in it, and we were told that tomorrow we'll play a game in this meadow, called "Capture the Flag."

After dinner, the whole camp got together up in the Quad and we had peanuts and Kool-aid, and there was a big bonfire and we sang songs. Then Mr. Taber, one of the counselors, said they were looking for kids with talent so there could be a High Pines Talent Show next Saturday night. There would be skits, music, jokes, anything at all, and so I reported that Paul Indian plays the piano, and they said that was fine since there is a piano locked up over at the mess hall, and so I hope Paul isn't angry that I said he could play. Then Mr. Warren said that one thing each cabin should do tonight is elect a Cabin Leader, and these Cabin Leaders should report first thing in the morning to their counselors.

Well, the funny thing is, once we got back to our cabins, Ham Pumpernil right away nominated me as Cabin Leader for our cabin, Number Nine. Bob Daly said, "Why him?" Ham said, "Because he's smart. He even brought books." And this seemed to impress the other kids, but Fred Elston said, "I think the oldest guy should be Cabin Leader." We asked who was oldest and it came out that Fred Elston would be fourteen in just over a month, and so he was nearly a year older than me. We voted on it and only Fred and I didn't vote, and it was a tie. So Bob McCarthy said, "Fred and Win ought to have a debate," and Fred said I would have to talk first, since I was nominated first.

So I said, "I don't know why I should be Cabin Leader, because I've never been a leader of anything before. On the other hand, in St. Matthew, Chapter 20, 1 to 16, there is a story telling how, in the Kingdom of Heaven, the last shall be the first, and the first shall be the last, so that maybe inexperience is a good thing, after all. Outside of that, I guess Fred Elston would be able to do anything I could do, and I don't see how I could debate with him at all, unless we have issues to debate about—like if we made special rules for our cabin, and disagreed about what the rules should be, then we could debate about that. But as it is, it's just a matter of whether you want him or me to be Cabin Leader."

"What do you mean, rules?" asked Ezra Finley.

"Who wants rules?" asked Willy Schunn.

"I was just trying to raise some issues for debating," I said.

"We have enough rules already," said Fred Elston. "What kind of rules would you make?"

"I don't know. Maybe they'd be like the rules of ancient Persia, because they were very simple. For example, everybody has to tell the truth. Then, nobody should owe money, because owing money leads to lies. Then, nobody gets punished for doing anything just once."

"That's a pretty wise rule," said Willy.

"Even the King," I said, "couldn't punish a man for doing something just once. And then, when there is any punishment, you always have to figure out the good things someone has done, too, so the punishment won't be too bad."

"What kind of rules would you make?" Willy asked Fred.

"Hell," said Fred, "who wants to debate? I'm going to vote for Weyn, too. Let him be Cabin Leader, I don't even want to be."

I said, "No swearing."

Fred looked at me grimly for a while but he didn't say anything about changing his vote, and so here I am, Cabin Leader Winston Weyn, so it hasn't been such a bad day, all in all.

Back to the Pentateuch, and then lights out.

JUNE 1

I found out that Paul Indian was elected Cabin Leader in the cabin next to ours, and at Number Seven George Meridel was elected, so we went together over to the mess hall to meet Edward Heinz.

The big guys were meeting their counselors, too, and I saw that, while neither Howard nor Pete Bunch was among them, Frank Reilley was there.

There wasn't much to talk about at the meeting, but I did ask Edward Heinz if it was all right to have special rules in our cabin, and I told him about the election and how we had needed some issues to debate. He asked, "What kind of rules?" I described the rules of ancient Persia I had in mind and he smiled kind of queerly and said he didn't care, but I had better check with him about imposing any rules, especially the ones involving punishments. I told him the only kind of punishment I had thought of for breaking any rule was to have a cabin kitty, and to have each kid who broke a rule put a nickel into the kitty each time, and then the whole cabin would divide up the kitty when it was time to go home.

George Meridel asked me, "Are you really going to have rules in your cabin?"

I said, "Maybe."

"It's a good idea," George said, nodding thoughtfully. "I'm going to make some rules for my cabin, too."

Then we moved over toward where the bigger guys were jabbering and they pretended not to notice us for a while, but finally this really big colored guy winked at us and George Meridel pretended to be scared and ran off a few feet. So the colored guy said, "I'm Don Egriss, Cabin Eleven," and he put his hand right out to me. "Maybe us Cabin Leaders ought to get to know each other." I thought this was a fine gesture, so I introduced myself. I guess I'll write all the names of the Cabin Leaders here, while I remember them. Starting with the smallest kids, Benny Wasserman is in Cabin Number One, he's ten. Hugh Flowers, Cabin Number Two and Walter Eidelman, Cabin Number Three, and Tom Nealey, Cabin Number Four, they're all either ten or eleven. Orlando Mills, they call him Orly, he's eleven and is Cabin Leader at Number Five. Jimmy Davids, Number Six. Then George Meridel, Number Seven; Paul Indian, Number Eight, and me in Number Nine. In the three cabins for the guys at least fourteen or older, it is Frank Reilley in Number Ten—he's sixteen or seventeen; Don Egriss in Number Eleven, the biggest guy in the camp, but I don't think he's as old as Frank Reilley; and another strange guy who is supposed to be a good friend of Frank Reilley, Stanley Runk in Number Twelve. They call him Runk the Punk.

Because there is so much swearing in my cabin, I announced today that each time a kid used a swear word, he would have to put a nickel in the cabin kitty. "The hell with that," said Bob Daly. And Fred Elston said, "I say the hell with that, too. This isn't a concentration camp, you jerk, and we don't have to take your rules, you son of a bitch, God damn it, hell,

31

and I don't owe you a dime." I told him he owed fifteen cents for that, at least. So Bob Daly shouted, "Hell, hell, hell, hell, hell!" There were five of them, I counted, and I said, "I didn't invent the rule about swearing, and if you'd rather go to The Brig, that's all right with me. If you'd rather pay up in the cabin kitty, just let me know." "No one is going to put *me* in The Brig for cussing, God damn it," said Fred Elston. "Same here," said Willy Schunn. So I pointed out how the kitty was a good idea, if they would think about it for a minute, because we'd all have some money to divide up at the end of our month at High Pines. And I told them that they elected me Cabin Leader, and the whole point of me being elected would be stupid if I didn't try to keep the rules, and I just thought it would be more fun to have money in the cabin kitty to divide up among everyone, than to always be reporting guys and seeing them go to The Brig. Well, some of the guys thought about this, and since Bob Daly and Fred Elston owed most of the money, the rest thought maybe I was right after all.

I told Paul Indian about this while we were going up to the meadow to play "Capture the Flag," and Paul said, "Hell, everybody swears, even the counselors." But that just made me a little mad, because it would be all the harder to try to keep rules if even the counselors broke them.

As Cabin Leaders, George Meridel and Paul and I tossed coins to see who would be the two captains of the "Capture the Flag" teams, and I and George became the captains. Edward Heinz was a kind of umpire, and the meadow was divided in half with a long rope stretched out across it, on the ground, just above the weeds, and each team had one half of the field. Anyone who crossed the rope could be captured by the other team, if he was tagged. The idea of the game was for one team to capture the "flag" of the other team, which was a big handkerchief laid out across the bushes at the farthest two ends of the field.

First we appointed guys to guard the flags (I appointed Eddy Hoag, who is in Paul's cabin, to guard our flag). Then we had to try to figure out how someone could get across the rope and clear down to the opposite end of the meadow to capture George's flag, and get it back again without being tagged. So what I did was to send a couple of guys out into the woods to see if they couldn't circle all the way around behind the meadow, and come up behind George's flag and get it that way.

Then, while those guys were off in the woods, I joined the rest of my team and tried to keep George's team from crossing into our half of the meadow. Pretty soon there was a big commotion behind me and I saw George had had the same idea and that one of his guys was trying to get our flag from behind, but we captured him, and then I went back to guarding the rope. Pretty soon I saw that the kid who kept going back and forth in front of me (it was kind of hard to tell who was guarding who) had this enormous sucker on a long stick and he seemed more interested in the sucker than in the game, and suddenly I got the idea to grab his sucker, which I did, and he was so surprised he couldn't hold on to it. I took it back a few steps so that he couldn't reach me, and he went red in the face and marched over the rope and snatched it back out of my hand, and I tagged him. He went redder and said, "You cheated." I said, "All is fair in love and war, and you're captured."

He insisted that he go and talk to Edward Heinz about it, which we did, and so Edward Heinz sized up this angry kid I captured, and then he sized me up, and at last he told the kid, "Well, it really does look like you're a prisoner." That was good news, so I took my prisoner off, even though I couldn't help having the feeling that Edward Heinz had decided in my favor because the other guy was bigger and it might not have been necessary for me to play at all if I couldn't use my brains in the game. I left my prisoner with Eddy Hoag and the other guards back at the flag, and returned to "the front line."

Pretty soon I saw that Bob McCarthy was a prisoner down at George's flag, and that Ezra Finley had come back, and so our plan had failed to work, just as George's had. So I went and had a conference with Paul and Eddy and a couple others, and it was Paul who suggested that we just ought to charge straight down the middle, all together, and someone would be bound to get the flag that way, especially if we worked it like football, using some of the guys to block George's team from tagging the kid assigned to capture George's flag. We decided this was probably a good idea, and so I sent Ezra Finley back into the woods again, to distract part of George's team to one side of the field, and then I sent another kid out into the woods on the other side, and this distracted another part of George's team, and then while George was trying to figure out what to do about the situation, our task force took off. I had assigned Paul to get the flag, but he said I should get it since I was captain, and I couldn't do much blocking anyhow, so I ran right in the middle of the task force, and we screamed like Indians, and Paul and I both got all the way down to George's flag and I grabbed the flag and, seeing a couple of George's men running toward me, I just kept running right into the woods, hoping to circle back through them to my side of the meadow, and I ran straight into a tree and hit my head so hard I fell down and got all dizzy. So I pushed the flag out to Paul and said, "Get going!" But he said, "Are you hurt?" I said, "Get going!" because George's guys were on top of us but Paul just stood there, so I got to my feet and began to run again, and these kids chased me all through the woods and it took me about ten minutes to get back to my side of the meadow. They were still chasing me then, so I just stopped and let them catch up with me and tagged them, and that confused them quite a bit, seeing that they had not only lost their flag but were prisoners, too. My team was very happy, and then I fainted.

I don't know what happened, I didn't feel anything, but suddenly I just heard a crazy buzzing sound, and maybe for only a second everything went spinning sick and black and then I don't remember a thing. Soon, Edward Heinz was bending over me and I said, "I hit a tree." Edward Heinz told me I had a lump and had to go and see the nurse. Bob McCarthy was laughing and he said, "Hey, you should have seen yourself run into that tree. *Wump!*" And he hit his head with his hand, crossed his eyes and fell down. Everyone laughed.

So, even though I protested against it, I had to go and see Miss Newman, the nurse, who told me I should run backward when I am looking that way. She is fat, but kind of nice.

Well, I see this is getting very long, but I could write more if it wasn't getting late. I enjoy writing and, reading back over what I have written, I see I have written it rather well, and so maybe I will be a writer when I grow up and work for a newspaper, like Uncle Giles.

Dinner tonight was spaghetti, salad, beets, milk, pie—quite good. Then we went to the marshmallow roast and some of the guys told jokes, and it was when the jokes started to get a little dirty that we had to come back to our cabins.

JUNE 2

They say you just can't please some people, which is certainly true, because at breakfast this morning Howard came over to our table and, for no reason at all, began to rib me because I am Cabin Leader. I guess he may be jealous, but he acts like he wouldn't be a Cabin Leader even if they drafted him and gave him a salary. Stanley Runk, and not Frank Reilley, as I had thought, is Cabin Leader where Howard is, but Frank's and Stanley's cabins are close and Frank and Stanley are good friends, and Fred Elston says the two groups always stick together and are pretty much like one cabin. As for Stanley, he may be a Cabin Leader, but he only makes fun of it, and I guess he was elected Cabin Leader mostly because everyone over there thought it would be a good joke on Stanley.

So when Howard went away, Ham Pumpernil said, "Is that guy really your brother?" And Frank Divordich said, "He doesn't like you too much, does he?" So I said, "He was only kidding around," but I was feeling very mad at Howard.

The boys having the best time up here, I think, are the smallest kids. They just do what they are told and don't have to be responsible about anything. The big guys act odd, they don't seem to care for High Pines at all. They slink around and manage to look like they haven't got anything to do even when they are doing things. After the meeting of Cabin Leaders this morning, Stanley Runk said that all the big guys were supposed to play "Capture the Flag" this morning and I couldn't say whether he laughed more about it, or groaned more. What the big guys say, even Frank Reilley, is: why did they have guys of sixteen and even seventeen come up here if all the entertainment is for twelve-year-olds?

I just don't understand Frank Reilley. He seems very nice one minute, but then he seems to be trying hard to prove he could never be nice, and tries to impress everyone with how tough he is. Sometimes he seems very kind and modest, and then he'll start walking around with a real swagger. But he uses big words and speaks quite good English, I think, and anyhow seems smarter than the guys he goes around with. When he isn't around those guys, then he speaks more softly and today he stood around with me a couple minutes and just seemed sad about something, and he talked about how pretty the sky was and gave me one of those careful grins and patted my head, and even asked me about what I was reading; but he didn't sound very interested in Herodotus when I talked about it. So he can be very nice, really. But Fred Elston told me how Frank got mad at this big kid named Mason, who is at least as big as Frank is, and Frank almost sent Mason to the ground just with shouting, and when Mason held his ground, Frank slapped him right across the face and was just shaking with fury. Mason was so impressed he didn't hit Frank back or anything, he just walked off. I sure wouldn't want him to be mad at me.

This morning I had to go back and see Miss Newman, to be sure I was all right, which I did while the other kids were swimming in the river. And a little later, what was far worse, I was down at the river myself, swimming, and Edward Heinz was there and he told me I was beginning to swim pretty well, but then Frank Divordich went and called out: "Hey, Mr. Heinz, Weyn's got a rash on his ass," and Edward Heinz said, "It isn't his ass, they're his buttocks, but," he looked down at me, "it's a rash, all right." I had been scratching back there and I tried to see what he was talking about, but couldn't, although I could feel I was kind of pimply. I said, "It's all right," and Edward Heinz went away. But before you know it, he came right back and had Miss Newman with him, and he may have been dressed but a lot of us guys weren't and so everyone went crashing into the water like she was a tiger, including me. Edward Heinz said to me, "Come on out here," and I said, "No," and he said, "Come on, Win," and I said, "No," and he said, "I want Miss Newman to see that rash, and you come on up here right now." So I had to back out of the river as carefully as I could and straight back to Miss Newman, like she was a garage and I was a car, and the guys just laughed and laughed to see me all bent over like that. It was terrible. After she examined me, I plunged back in like I was All-American swimming champion of the year, and once Miss Newman and Edward Heinz had gone away, I was dumb enough to begin acting like one, too, because I swam over to where the water was too deep for me.

I don't remember swimming into that deep part of the river, but all at once I was aware that everything was heavier and darker and greener and I looked up and it just looked like water on top of water above me, and suddenly I was too scared and just forgot how to swim. I started to kick and push my arms around crazily—I didn't hurt or anything but things were going green and black, and I was drinking water down there and it was Don Egriss who came over and got hold of me and tugged me away, so he saved my life, I believe he really did. He got me out of the water and sat with me until I got my breath back and you would think that I would have said, "Thank you," to Don Egriss, but I was too ashamed. I just felt like I could never admit I was drowning and so I told him I was flailing around that way on purpose, to see if anyone could try to save me. I guess he knows I lied and I am more ashamed of the lie than I was ashamed of being such a bad swimmer, but I don't know how to tell him I lied. So far, no one has said anything about this, so I guess Don Egriss didn't say anything to anyone about it, and that was very nice of him.

Today, after swimming, we had to play baseball. Here, I was very lucky because, like in "Capture the Flag," I got to be captain of one of the teams, and as captain I didn't have to make myself play. Paul was the captain of the other team, and his team won, 10-6.

After lunch, two big kids were hanging around our cabin, Jerome Blackridge (I have never seen him smile) and Manuel Rivaz (who is nearly always smiling). They were over here because Fred Elston knows them, and they said that the boys' camp was dull because it was full of boys, so they meant to skip out through the woods to take a look at the girls' camp down the river. They asked Fred if he wanted to go along, and Bob Daly said he wanted to go, too. "If it's against the rules," Bob told me with a sneer, "I'll give you a nickel, just charge it to my account." So the four of them left, snickering like evil villains in an old television movie.

Well, I should say that I gave some time to trying to decide whether I should report those guys for breaking camp rules. First of all, I am Cabin Leader, and if I don't show responsibility, then I'm not a good Cabin Leader, and I can't understand why anyone would think I'd care to be a *bad* Cabin Leader. Of course, this is the kind of attitude a lot of kids don't like, who say that a guy is only supposed to be responsible to his friends, and never to rules; but then if a guy is only loyal to his friends and not to rules, the whole business of rules is silly. And if the rules are silly, I'd just rather not be Cabin Leader at all. The idea of reporting, I guess, is to keep bad things from happening, but I see on television that even cops hate informers, it's like treason and nobody likes a sneak, so nobody tells on people, especially their friends. Well, I didn't report them, and that's the point. But I can't say I feel I did right by not "informing."

I have written all this to explain why I did what I did tonight, when all the guys were together in my cabin. I told them I didn't like the idea of sneaking on them, but that leaving the camp area, especially to go to the girls' camp, was a serious violation of the rules, and it was not to happen again. I tried to speak very sternly.

Bob Daly said, "Oh it won't happen again, Cabin Leader, sir, at least not until we decide to go over there again."

Ham Pumpernil, who nearly always sides with me, said, "What's the matter, Daly? Can't you keep away from the girls?"

Bob Daly said, "Keep out of it, Ham Sandwich, or I'll cut you in two and feed you to the minnows."

Ham was just beside himself—I hadn't realized he could get mad like that—and he said, "Who are you talking to?"

"You," Bob Daly stuck his face into Ham's, "I'm

talking to you, Sandwich, Ham-head, Ass-head, Peanut Butter."

"That's five cents," I told Bob Daly.

"For what?" he turned on me. "Peanut butter?"

"No, for the other," I said.

"That Manuel Rivaz," laughed Fred Elston, like nothing else was going on, "he went and made a date with a girl for tonight. They're going to see each other up in the woods somewhere."

"Hey," said Willy Schunn. "Did you guys really see some girls?"

"What do you think we saw at the girls' camp?" asked Bob Daly. "The United States Congress?"

"He means did you see them swimming?" asked Ezra Finley.

"Sure we saw them swimming," said Frank Divordich, "and there is this one girl who don't walk at all, she's so fat, she kind of gets her feet moving and then her weight just carries her along."

I don't know why, but Divordich talking like that about a girl he wasn't supposed to be looking at in the first place just made me mad, and I said, "Well, if you guys go outside the camp again, I'll report you, and that's that."

"Aw, keep your bones on," said Willy Schunn.

"What an Ass-head," muttered Bob Daly.

"I'm keeping track, Bob," I told him, "don't think I'm not. That's another nickel you owe the cabin kitty."

Then I just left the cabin and went over to talk to Paul for a while.

I guess Paul and I are friends again. I think he was peeved with me for grabbing that flag out of his hand and running with it at the end of yesterday's game of "Capture the Flag." But he hasn't said anything about it, and tonight we talked about the Talent Show on Saturday night, and he said he was going to play a sonatina by a man named Kuhlau, pronounced *koo-low*. He said he could play things by Mozart and Bach, but this particular piece is pretty fast and so he thought it would be better liked up here. I told him I would rather have him play Bach, since Bach is my favorite composer and I have frequently heard his music on the radio. This is because Bach sounds like morning. Now and then, he sounds like sunset, but he never sounds like night. The music of Beethoven, I think, sounds like sunset and night, nearly always, and since I favor morning as a pleasant time of day, I guess that's why I like Bach.

This afternoon I read underneath a tree for a while, and Don Egriss came and sat beside me, and I felt very embarrassed. I wanted to tell him I was sorry I had lied to him, but I couldn't get it out of my mouth, and so I went on reading. He asked me what I was reading after a while, so I told him it was Herodotus, and he laughed at that like he thought I was reading it in Greek or something. "You read a lot?" I asked him. "Kid," he shook his head and grinned funnily, like he was embarrassed instead of me, "I get bad grades in television, what do I want with books?" This disappointed me, somehow, and I suppose I had been hoping he would like books. He said he was in the eleventh grade and then he frowned and said, "That sure looks like a hard book for a peanut like you." "I like hard books," I told him. He shrugged and said, "Well, I wish I was a clever guy like Reilley and could talk like I'd read every book in the world, but I'm me and I don't mean to take issue with God about it." "Do you believe in God?" I asked. "Sure," he nodded, "don't you?" I didn't say anything, and then I asked if Frank Reilley was really clever. Don Egriss shrugged again and told me, "Well, he's a little too cocky for me, Reilley is, but he gets his A's, okay, so who am I to call him dumb? Hey now," he stood up, "you take it easy on them books." I guess that bothered me a little, him suggesting maybe I shouldn't read too much, or maybe I was just looking embarrassed again, but he began to look confused and then turned and kind of hurried away.

I wish I had had the courage to tell him thank you for having saved my life. Well, I will have to do that before leaving here.

JUNE 3

The whole morning for Cabin Nine was spent in the ping-pong room, off the Administration Building, and in four games I made about six points. I was pretty dismal by the time we finished.

George Meridel has gone nuts on the subject of rules. At the Cabin Leaders' meeting this morning, he said he had made these rules:

(1) No leaving Cabin Seven until he said so.
(2) No starting to eat at the table until he was seated.
(3) His guys all have to say the Pledge of Allegiance every morning, as soon as they get out of bed.

George said these rules were to keep order in Cabin Seven, and that order is a good thing, but of course he is only being mean and dumb. I have begun to wonder if George was elected Cabin Leader only because he can beat up everyone in his cabin. Well, Stanley Runk got a big kick out of George's announcement and he told George that he ought to have the kids in Cabin Seven salute him whenever they happened to pass him, and I do believe George took him seriously, he just nodded slowly and seemed to ponder it. That amused Stanley no end, and he chortled and chuckled and began to describe George and me as Camp Cops, and said: "Look out, you guys, here come the Camp Cops. Mind your rules, everybody, the Camp Cops will get you," and then Stanley became angry all at once: "God damn little finks, why don't you go back to the traffic patrol at your schools?"

"Dry up," muttered Paul Indian.

"What was that?" Stanley wheeled on Paul, looking amazed. "You speaking to me, little fellow?"

"Shut up about cops," Paul scowled at him. "My dad is a cop."

"You a cop's kid?" Stanley asked, pointing straight at him.

"That's right," Paul said, going red, "and shut up about cops, damn it."

Well, it just seemed funny to Stanley that there should be a real live son of a policeman at High Pines, so again he began to laugh. What a place!

I went back to suggesting that George Meridel change his rules. "You'll get those guys at your cabin all mad at you," I told him, "and they'll revolt."

"Revolt!" screamed Stanley Runk, tears running out of his eyes. "Hahhh! Revolt!" He shrieked for a time, so there was nothing to do but watch him. "Hahhrarharh!" He had to sit down on one of the benches.

Paul went away, so I did too.

After lunch (beans), we went on a long hike again. Mostly, we covered ground we had already covered, but it was nice even so. Edward Heinz said that tomorrow, Saturday, we'll go in another direction and we're going to catch butterflies and that he'll show us how to mount them and identify them. He said it is very interesting, and maybe some of us would even begin a real butterfly collection after seeing how much fun it is.

I am a moralist. There it is. So I asked Paul Indian

how he felt about collecting butterflies, since after all butterflies are fairly innocent creatures and don't hurt anything, unless they are swarms of crop butterflies— ordinarily they just go about looking pretty. But Paul just said, "There are plenty of butterflies."

"That's not the idea," I told him. "It's just that maybe we shouldn't kill something simply for the fun of it."

"Well, it's not just for fun. It's to study them and collect them."

"That's just making a hobby out of it, and hobbies are fun," I said.

"My God," Paul scowled at me, "they're only butterflies."

"I heard somewhere that Albert Schweitzer didn't even kill wasps," I told Paul.

"Weyn, you're nuts. Go talk to Edward Heinz if you want to get philosophical, will you?"

So I did. I told Edward Heinz everything I had told Paul, but Edward Heinz just kind of chuckled about it and said, "What have you been reading, Win?" Then, before I could answer, he became serious and said, "Nature is a violent thing, young man. Maybe some individuals are saintly enough to stand apart from nature, but most people aren't individuals, and most of nature won't be pacified. Do you really feel bad about killing butterflies?"

"They don't hurt anybody. And they're very pretty."

"Well, I think you're being a little finicky," Edward Heinz said, "and I think you'll regret it if you don't go along with us, but I won't force you to if you don't want to."

So that was the end of that. I don't know whether I should chase butterflies or not. I can understand studying things for scientific reasons, of course, but I can't figure out if it is right to kill something which is harmless just to know something about it.

After we got back from our hike, we found out there had been a fight in the camp between some of the big guys, and one guy was actually in The Brig. I, Paul, Ham and Bob McCarthy went down together to The Brig, and a few guys were standing around there, laughing and joking, and I saw the guy looking out from between the bars at the window of The Brig was John Mason. I don't know what all the joking was about but Pete Bunch was there and he was making some crack about how John Mason wouldn't have gone all the way to the girls' camp when Miss Newman was at High Pines or something like that.

Fred Elston and Frank Divordich came along and Fred said, "Who is it?"

"John Mason," said Ham.

Pete Bunch suddenly caught sight of me and said, "Look who's here, it's Cabin Leader Winnie Pooh. That explains it. Miss Newman wasn't here, but Cabin Leader Winnie Pooh was here and needed the money for his famous cabin kitty. How's your pussy, Winnie?"

This made a lot of guys laugh, it was awfully funny after all, and then Don Egriss came sauntering up and John Mason called out: "Egriss, Egriss! Come on in here, Egriss, you ape, you monkey! Let the monkey back in his cage. The whole thing's a terrible mistake! Hey Egriss, you ought to be in here, not me. You're responsible, you're a real boy scout, a Cabin Leader. Me, what am I? A bum, a killer, a delinquent. Egriss, you didn't protect me from myself. Hey, when I get out of here, you're going to have to protect *you* from myself." He made a few more cutting remarks like that, aimed at Don Egriss, which I couldn't understand at all, since it seems to me Don is friendly toward everyone; but then Paul or someone did mention something about Don not getting along very well with John Mason and a few other guys, and I guess it is because Don is a Negro. Anyhow, Don went away and I kind of felt like going after him, but I just couldn't understand the situation, so in another minute I just went off with Paul and Ham and Bob.

John Mason was supposed to be in The Brig until lights out tonight, and I guess he will be out pretty soon.

Just like it wasn't merry enough seeing John Mason in The Brig today, Paul and Ham and I were walking through the trees behind the smallest kids' cabins after dinner and saw old Stanley Punk Runk there, with his huge hunting knife, which he was throwing into a pine trunk. He would throw it, then go up and pull it out and go back and throw it again, and we watched him long enough to see he could stick it in nearly every time. "Well well," said Stanley, yanking out his knife and finally observing us after we had been standing there for what seemed hours, "here are the troopers. Did I do a bad thing and you come to report me, Winnie Pooh? You got to give me another chance. I'll go straight, cop's boy, you got to believe me"—this last being aimed at Paul.

Stanley tossed the knife again, real carelessly, and *ssskkthnk!* it stood quivering in the trunk of the pine.

"Hey," said Ham to Stanley, "what's that guy Mason in The Brig for?"

"Butterflies," said Stanley the Punk, pulling his knife out of the tree and wiping the blade on his trousers.

Ham laughed. "You mean he flipped? He's got butterflies where his brains should be?"

Stanley examined his knife and again wiped it on his trouser leg. "No, small crap, that ain't what I mean," he said cordially. "I mean he didn't take to the idea of skipping up mountain trails, giggling with joy at the thought of waving his little net over a cute little black and yellow butterbug. The idea just never took him. Me neither." Since no one said anything, Stanley finally went on, "We were supposed to spend practically a whole day running after butterflies. Can you beat it? Not just chasing them, but *capturing* them. Not just capturing them, but learning *how* to capture them. And then we would sit down and talk about them and read about them and it'd be all dandy. What a joint. Butterbugs. Nets. Don't this place drag?" He shook his head and sneered, but then chuckled and it came out like a sneeze. "So there we were," he spread his arms out, the knife shining pinkish from the sunset, "the big hunters out in the woods, stealing cautiously through the brush, nets at the ready, when all at once Mason caught something. He caught something! Right in his net! It was Dick Richardson. So then we all began to catch each other instead of butterbugs and we broke a couple nets. Call Scotland Yard! Taber told us to quiet down or we just couldn't chase any more butterflies. Now, that sobered us. That really sobered us. What a creep."

"Who?" asked Ham. "Mr. Taber?"

"He's a creep all right, he's a butterfly himself. Hell, we just went right on horsing around. I mean, who the hell wants to catch butterflies? Do they taste good or something? So Mason, he got hold of Dick Richardson again and brought him down like a hippo, you know? That Richardson," Stanley gave us his soprano chuckle again, "mad? You'd have thought his pants were on fire, he really tore into Mason. So old Taber says that's the end of the butterfly hunt, and us without a single trophy; man, we were all broken up about it. So Taber tries to get Mason off Richardson, but Mason is a little mad himself by now and just from his knees, mind you, he gives one straight at Taber's jaw that nearly sent Taber to Disneyland. Laugh? Thought I'd die, thought my pants would never dry, but Taber didn't get the joke at all. So Mason gets eight hours in The Brig. Richardson has to spend an hour or two in there, too. Tomorrow morning." All of a sudden, he flung his knife again and it went whizzing and pinging into the pine trunk, quivering. "This whole place is full of butterflies, if you ask me. It don't fly, it flutters."

Paul said, "Why'd you come to High Pines, anyhow?"

Stanley just shrugged. "I had nothing else to do, cop's boy. Anyhow, my old man made me come. What's it to you?"

At the bonfire at the Quad tonight, instead of singing, we had a long speech on responsibility and citizenship by Mr. Warren, and he also spoke of God, and it seemed to him that responsibility and citizenship had more to do with God than anything else. He sounded like Mama and the Reverend Munson talking at once, in a way, and then he said that the butterfly chase for my own group of cabins was canceled, since so many of the bigger boys had found it unpleasant. He said it was too bad, since we would probably have enjoyed it very much, and this was one way in which a few people could hurt many people by not abiding by the law. I guess it was because some of the bigger guys thought it was wrong to put Mason and Richardson in The Brig that Mr. Warren also pointed out it is possible to be expelled from High Pines.

Anyhow, this is how my own problem about whether

I should kill butterflies or not was solved. Now I won't have to think about it right away.

After Mr. Warren's speech, he had us all sing *Hail Hail, the Gang's All Here,* and then he reminded us that tomorrow night there'll be the Talent Show, and then we came back to our cabins.

JUNE 4

Right after getting up this morning, I began to hear a kind of chanting from George Meridel's cabin, so I went over to listen, and I looked in and saw they were all saying the Pledge of Allegiance. They had no flag, but George Meridel was holding up a handkerchief, like the whole thing was the introduction ceremony to a game of "Capture the Flag," and if that wasn't enough, no sooner had they finished with the Pledge of Allegiance than they began on *The Star Spangled Banner*.

After they finished singing, I asked George if singing the National Anthem was one of his rules, and he looked at me suspiciously and said, "You have rules at your cabin, so don't butt into my cabin."

Later, I asked one of the guys in George's cabin and he said it didn't matter to him if they said the Pledge of Allegiance and sang the National Anthem every morning, and that it was at least patriotic, and George had said he wondered just why any kid in his cabin would *not* want to say the Pledge of Allegiance or sing the National Anthem every morning, and when George put it that way, no one had been able to think of why they might not want to have those rules.

Well, I still have rules troubles in my own cabin, since it is hard to keep the kitty paid up. Bob Daly still owes twenty cents, and the kitty will have eighty cents in it when he pays up, which is a dime apiece for everyone in the cabin. When I pointed out how the kitty is progressing, the guys were more and more on my side about it and Frank Divordich and Ezra Finley both paid their nickels in this morning, which didn't bother them too much because they know they will have at least a dime, and probably more, coming back out of it at the end of the month.

At the Cabin Leaders' meeting this morning, Edward Heinz made a point of asking us how we were getting on with our rules, and George looked at me like I might have said something to Edward Heinz already, and then he described how the guys in his cabin had to say the Pledge of Allegiance and sing the National Anthem in the morning. Edward Heinz really looked perplexed at that and asked George, "What's the idea behind all that, George?" So George mumbled and grimaced a bit about order and patriotism. Edward Heinz nodded and asked how George's cabin feels about the rules. George said they all liked the rules fine, all except for one kid, named Lenny Kistner, because he couldn't sing in tune. Edward Heinz said that George shouldn't force Lenny Kistner to sing if he didn't want to, and George looked glum about it, like he thought Lenny Kistner should sing even if he was mute, if George told him to; and Edward Heinz also said George shouldn't make the boys follow those rules unless they really wanted to, since it was not George's right to decide when or where those things should be done. George said, "All right," and managed not to salute.

Actually, the Cabin Leaders' meetings have gone kind of stale, because there is never much to say once Edward Heinz has told us what we'll do each day. None of the Cabin Leaders seem to have much to say to each other, either; as Cabin Leaders, I mean. I guess the big kids are right when they say it's all kind of silly. So we were just standing around after the meetings today, listening to Stanley Runk tell Frank Reilley that Dick Richardson, who was fighting with John Mason yesterday, is supposed to spend an hour in The Brig before lunch. The big guys don't like this treatment because it's too much like being sent to their rooms by their folks or something, but in another way they don't mind it because it seems kind of crazy to be behind bars for a while.

Then Frank Reilley said, "I'll tell you this much, though. I think they ought to let Rivaz alone."

Someone asked what Frank meant by that, and Stanley Runk threw his arms up and said, "Rivaz is next," and he gave Paul Indian a kind of smelly look, "and I'm just betting someone squealed on him about May."

May is this girl Manuel Rivaz was supposed to see, I guess everyone knew her name, and I gathered Mr. Warren had found out about it.

Don Egriss said, "Well, he ought to have stayed where he belonged."

For some reason, that made Frank Reilley angry. He turned his mad purplish eyes on Don and said, "That's not fair, Egriss. Who knows a nicer guy than Rivaz? Did he ever hurt anyone? Anyone at all? If it was Jerry Blackridge, even Runk here, I could see how they might have got aggravated."

"Who, me?" squeaked Runk the Punk. "I don't aggravate nobody!"

"But Rivaz," Frank went on, "the only thing he did was make a little fun for himself. He didn't involve anyone except one gal who asked for the involvement. And they'll probably give him worse than they gave

John Mason." Suddenly Frank was looking right at me. "I hate stupidity," he announced, "especially in adults. If they didn't want a good-looking, cheerful kind of a guy like Rivaz to find a girl, they shouldn't have built their camps so close together. Or else they should have strung barbed wire around them. Or maybe they should have rules about no kids as good-looking as that being allowed at High Pines."

"Hey," said Stanley, "tonight's that dumb show. Why don't we go on over to the girls' camp while the cop's boy's pinkies are picking at the piano?"

"As long as you're going out," Don Egriss shook his head, "why don't you just keep on going home? You guys aren't doing yourselves or anyone else any good up here."

"Look, Egriss," Frank began.

"That goes for you too, Reilley," Don said very nastily, and he suddenly looked like he never had liked Frank—he almost shook he was so mad at Frank. "You with all your brains, your A's, your speeches at school, man, you could afford to stand apart a little, you could . . ."

"Shut up, Don," Frank said.

"You could put some of those brains into . . ."

"Shut up, Don!" Frank said again.

Don shut up. I was very surprised. He just stopped looking mad and began to look sad, and then Don walked away, and I still don't understand how Frank could tell Don to shut up that way, since Don is so much bigger.

Stanley Runk was still saying he wanted to go to the girls' camp during the Talent Show, but Frank Reilley said it wasn't a good idea.

"Well, I'm resigning as Cabin Leader," said Stanley in disgust—because he was disgusting, I guess. "It's the only right thing to do. It was an unfair election. I rigged it. Now I got to cleanse my conscience, so I resign."

"What an unspirited attitude towards the well-being of the camp community," said Frank Reilley with a grin which warmed everything between his nose and his chin. "Didn't you hear the good word from Citizen Warren last night, Mr. Punk?"

"Are you kidding?" Stanley squeaked. "Man, I was counting pine needles. I counted nearly a thousand pine needles while Warren was slobbering up there."

Frank Reilley went grim again and said, "Warren should be smarter than to send guys as big as Mason and Richardson out chasing butterflies. If there's one thing I can't stand, it's dumbness in people over twenty. This place could use a little leadership, I'll tell you."

"Hey, Indian," Stanley Punk Runk said kind of gloomily, "where did you get a name like Indian? You a family of savages or something?"

George Meridel giggled at that and said, "Sure, Crows. Like Egriss," and he giggled some more.

It was a grand meeting.

Since our butterfly chase was called off, we had some free time and Paul said, "You want to hike over and see what the girls' camp looks like?"

"Are you kidding?"

He shrugged. "I'm going. You want to go or not?"

"We're Cabin Leaders."

But he just said, "Tootie fruitie," and I couldn't think of anything to say to that.

"Besides," I told him, "we don't even know how to get there."

"Divordich knows."

"What do you want to go over there for?" I asked him.

"Look, I'm just tired of being shoved around."

"What do you mean?"

"I don't mean anything. We don't have anything else to do. Go on, go see if Divordich wants to come with us."

Paul was peeved, so I went and found Frank Divordich and I asked him if he knew how to get to the girls' camp.

"Sure," he said, "what's it to you?"

I asked him if he wanted to go over there with Paul and me, but it felt very funny to ask that. Divordich pointed out that it was against the rules to go over there, throwing that up in my face, so I told him he would be with two Cabin Leaders and wouldn't be responsible. It sounded like bad logic to me, but anyhow he sauntered along with me and then all three of us set out up the hill, into the woods.

While we were walking, Paul said, "That Meridel guy makes me sick."

"Why?" I asked, as though I didn't know that Meridel was a germ from my own experience.

"If he had his way," Paul said, "those guys in his cabin would be making his bed and polishing his shoes. For the sake of order."

I laughed, but Paul went on: "You, too. What did you have to think up rules for?"

"I didn't mean rules like George means rules," I said.

"That Runk makes me sick, too," Paul kind of snorted.

"Runk the Punk," laughed Frank Divordich.

"Don't let a guy like that get you down," I said, not wanting Paul to get in any fights with a guy who carried a big hunting knife. "Getting mad at him is like getting mad at a rock."

"Listen, though," said Frank Divordich, "I'll tell you something: some guys are too smart for their own good."

"Now, what does *that* mean?" asked Paul.

"I wasn't talking to you," said Divordich.

"Well, it's no news to me," I said, "because my brother is telling me that all the time. Of course, I still help him with his homework sometimes."

Divordich bowed down and pointed one hand at me and cried, "The Genius!"—like he was introducing some kind of freak at a circus.

It was a terribly long way and all through bushes and around hilly paths. It took I don't know how long to get where we were going, moving pretty quickly too. Of course, it was the only way to go, since we couldn't just go out of the front of the camp and down the road to the place where you enter the girls' camp. But we were feeling quite bedraggled by the time we came to the crest of this big hill which looks right down on the girls' camp.

It looked a lot like our camp, even to the turn of the river, except that there were a lot of prettier paths, with rocks sort of placed along them, while our paths are just dirt. And I saw that some of the cabins have curtains at the windows. There were a lot of girls swimming in the river and we watched them awhile from where we were lying underneath some shrubs.

"They're all wearing bathing suits," I said after a time.

Frank Divordich said, "What did you expect?"

I hadn't thought about it, really, but I had expected maybe that it would be the same as at the boys' camp.

"The thing is," said Divordich, "they must bathe sometime. Or do they take baths right in their swimsuits?"

"None of them have any soap or towel," Paul said, "and I don't see anyone scrubbing. Maybe they have showers some place."

There were, I guess, twenty or more girls swimming in the river, screaming and splashing, and five or six more lying beside the river, to get a suntan probably.

"Hey!" Frank Divordich got excited, "there's that big one again, there she is!" He pointed toward this very fat girl as she waddled up out of the water. "She was there last time, too."

"Boy," said Paul, "that's about the fattest girl I ever saw. I wonder how much she weighs."

"Look at her shake," old Divordich said gleefully.

Paul just said, "She can't help it," and this made Divordich giggle a little more. Then we watched for awhile until Paul said, "Well, we better go."

"Why don't we wait awhile?" asked Divordich. "Because maybe some of them will come to bathe."

"We better head back," Paul said. "It'll be time for lunch before we even get back. I don't want to be missed."

When we got back, I was mad at Frank Divordich right away, because the first thing he did was tell Bob Daly where we'd gone, and Bob Daly just cocked his head and looked at me like I had picked up a pretty curious smell out in the woods. "Well, just don't talk to me about rules any more," he said, "because, Winnie Pooh, I'm not listening." "Winnie Pooh," laughed Frank Divordich, and it was easy to see that you don't make friends with a guy just by breaking a rule with him. So I said, "I don't care what you do about rules, it's your business," and I took my Herodotus book and went to sit down by the river and read until lunch, because we had got back earlier than we thought it was. I had time to read for about fifteen minutes, but I couldn't think about Herodotus because I was feeling bad about having broken the rules, and of course that would mean the end of the rules in our cabin, and the kitty, and even the end of my ability to be a good Cabin Leader. I even felt a little mad with Paul, since it was his idea to go over to the girls' camp, but I guess I must have been curious, myself, because I went, after all, so it wasn't all Paul's fault. But I was mad at him, anyhow.

At lunch things got a little worse, which I am beginning to think they can always do, because Jerome Blackridge came over to our table and pushed his eyes around awhile and glowered and said, "Which one of you kids squealed on Rivaz?" Edward Heinz was just flabbergasted, I think, to see Blackridge put that question to us like that, and he said, "You get on back to your own table, Jerry, or I'm going to be doing some squealing myself." Blackridge looked back at Edward Heinz with a funny expression, it was both mean and questioning, he looked like there might have been ninety or a hundred things Edward Heinz could have squealed on him about, and he wasn't sure just which one Edward Heinz had in mind. But he finally went back to his table.

And after lunch Blackridge and Runk and a whole group began on us again, and when they got to me and Paul, good old Divordich said: "Hell, these guys could be expelled for the same reason. They've been over to the girls' camp themselves," and then we found out Manuel Rivaz was being expelled from High Pines and that's why the bigger kids were so upset about it. They thought it was unfair, because it would even get Manuel Rivaz in trouble at his home, as well as up here. Anyhow, when Runk bent his face down into mine, I don't mind admitting I was a little scared, and I said, "I didn't say anything to anyone."

Then Don Egriss sort of shoved the Punk away from me and said, "Stop making easy odds for yourself, Runk. If you're that nervous, just look my way. I'm here."

So Stanley hissed at him, "Maybe it was you, Egriss. Maybe you squealed on Rivaz."

"Now, don't you just wonder?" muttered Don, dead-pan, his hands on his hips.

Stanley looked up at Don for a while, then growled and meandered away and Blackridge tagged after him.

Of course, I myself think it is too bad they want to expel Manuel Rivaz, since he is always nice to people. But I will write more about this in a minute.

First let me put down, before I forget, and while I am on such happy subjects, that Ham Pumpernil got into a fight with Bob Daly today. I don't know how it started, but I know Ham won the fight. It was pretty good, because from the way Bob Daly talks and acts, one would figure he must be a good fighter. But Ham made him say uncle three times on the floor before he would let Daly up, and now people look at Ham with a new respect, including me.

Now, it was after this fight that George Meridel came in to say there was a special meeting called of Cabin Leaders and a few other guys, and I was supposed to go with Paul Indian, but he was rehearsing for the Talent Show. I asked George what the meeting was about, but he just said I had better come. So I invited Ham to go with me, and we followed George way up to the meadow, which seemed a crazy place for a meeting, but that's where it was. Stanley the Punk was there, with Frank Reilley and Blackridge and John Mason and Dick Richardson, and I saw even Manuel Rivaz was there—a whole bunch of big guys. Even Don Egriss. Also there were my brother, Howard, Pete Bunch, Eddy Hoag, who was supposed to be rehearsing something himself, Gogo Burns, I guess about sixteen or seventeen guys in all.

Frank Reilley was in charge of the meeting, it seemed, and he looked nervous for a while, then said, "Gather around, you guys, sit down. Sit down, Egriss." But Don said, "I ain't weary." "Aw, sit down," barked Frank Reilley, "we're going to be here awhile. Hey, Weyn, you should have brought Elston along. He'd be interested in this." Most of us were sitting down in the weeds and flowers, and Frank Reilley and Stanley Runk stayed on their feet. Frank spread his legs apart, put his thumbs in his belt, and looked out at us with a strange sort of face, almost like he was about to preach, and if he was trying to impress us he succeeded pretty well when he said, "There's going to be a revolution." Nobody said anything. I don't think anybody understood what he meant. I certainly didn't. Eventually someone was bound to say: "What do you mean?" "I mean," said Frank Reilley, "that we've got to do something to give this place a little action, we've got to stop seeing our buddies getting pushed around just because they've committed the crime of no longer being ten; we've got to save Rivaz from being expelled and getting in a jam with his folks. We've been talking it over, me and Runk, Mason, Richardson, Blackridge, we've talked it over and here's what we decided: we're taking over this whole camp."

"Why?" asked Don Egriss. "Just to save Rivaz?"

"Why?" Frank Reilley sounded like he couldn't find

any logic in the question at all. "Well, I'll tell you why in a word even you can understand, Egriss. For fun. That's why. It's fun not to be shoved. It's fun to know you don't have to be expelled. It's fun knowing you can be as old as we are without having to pretend like you're really eleven. It's fun. Does that answer your question?" He didn't wait for Don to say anything, but went on, "The thing is, if it's going to be a good revolution, if it's going to take, then we need plenty of cooperation. We have to plan and we need cooperation."

"I still don't see why you're talking about a revolution," said Don Egriss. "I can see you'd want to help Rivaz, if you can, but a *revolt*. Man, what are you revolting against?"

"Against the butterflies, Egriss," said Stanley Runk, "against the birdies, against the slow pace, the drag, Warren, Talent Shows, marshmallows, tiddlywinks. You drugged or something? Look, it's kicks. Nobody expected you to be interested, see? But you pipe up about this to anybody, fellow, and you're in The Brig with Warren. You understand?"

"My gosh," someone asked, "are you going to put Mr. Warren in The Brig?" I think it was Gogo Burns.

"Listen," said Frank Reilley, "no one is going to get hurt. That's all you have to remember. It won't hurt Warren to spend a bit of time in The Brig, especially if it's going to help Rivaz."

"How is it going to help Rivaz?" asked my brother, Howard.

"You leave that to us," Frank Reilley said. "You leave that to us for the moment. It will."

Manuel Rivaz said, "Just remember that helping me ain't the point of this revolution, though. I don't care about being helped that bad, and this thing wasn't my idea. All I say is, if you guys are doing it anyhow, I guess I'll be in on the fun. What the hell, I'm being expelled anyhow, so I got nothing to lose."

Frank Reilley went on about how the revolution would work, and how everyone would have some fun for as long as it lasted, and when I asked what kind of fun, he all at once looked at me and his cheeks got purple like his eyes and he said almost quietly, "I thought you were smart." I felt very dumb. "I thought you were smart," he said, "but I'll tell you what I mean. Fun is *doing things*. And when you're doing things for a good reason, then that's *really* fun. I figure that putting together a revolution, so long as we mean it in fun and aren't hurting anyone, is going to be a good time, and I figure that helping Rivaz and maybe quite a few of us, really, makes the good time a *very* good time. I like books, too, kid," he nodded at me, "but books are about doing things, aren't they? Let's not live our whole lives in between the covers."

"Hey, what's so wrong with that?" laughed Dick Richardson.

"Okay, you know what I mean," Frank Reilley said, and he gave his cheeks time to go back to their natural color, and then explained all the things they had to do in the revolution. They would have to capture Mr. Warren and the counselors and take charge of the "communications center" (there is one telephone, and he also included the public address equipment in "communications center"), and they would have to capture the cooks and Miss Newman, too, so she couldn't report on the revolution at the girls' camp. Frank talked quite awhile and said the whole thing was a lot like "Capture the Flag," really, except it was for big boys, and the revolution wouldn't be over until the whole of High Pines was in complete control of the revolution.

After some quiet, Don Egriss sort of sighed himself to his feet and said, "You better count me out."

"Okay," Frank Reilley nodded, "that's okay. You can count yourself out. Like Runk says, we expected it. We figured you should be in, you're a Cabin Leader after all, and so we gave you a chance. But, Egriss, you mutter a word to anyone, just to anyone at all, and you're in trouble. You hear me?"

Don stared at Frank, but Frank stared back, even harder, even more fiercely, and Don was the first one to look away.

All at once, then, Stanley Runk threw his arms up in the air and his hands seemed to shake at the ends of them like he had no control over them, and he shouted at us: "Are there any other guys here who'd rather stalk the wild flutter-butterbug?"

Well, that stirred the group a little, some guys laughed and we shifted our positions and Frank Reilley very quickly took count of us, and only Don Egriss came out with words all against the revolution. I was going to say something against it, but Frank Reilley told me, "I'm counting on you, Cabin Leader Winston Weyn. You're a smart kid"—he said that right out in front of everyone—"and we need you. You understand? You going to betray us?"

I shook my head. "I wasn't going to betray you," and then Frank just moved over to Ham, and so I guess in that way I had joined the revolution.

Frank passed through the gathering personally, drafting people into his revolution with his really intense eyes and his hands which squeezed shoulders and arms, and then he went back to stand in front of us.

"From now on," he announced, "everyone here except Don Egriss is part of what I'm calling the Revolutionary Committee. Indian and Elston will be invited to join this Committee. Now, tomorrow is visitors' day at High Pines, and we're going to have a lot of strangers walking around the camp. But Manuel Rivaz is expected to be on a bus out tomorrow, so we can't wait. We'll meet again tomorrow morning, all of us, at six o'clock, and you'll all get instructions then. Six o'clock. Be here. Weyn, tell Indian and Elston. Members of the Revolutionary Committee, are there any questions?"

For my part, I didn't dare to think of any questions. Frank Reilley might as well have asked me to ask questions about the possibility of invading China tomorrow morning. Stanley Runk brought out his knife and began to throw it against a tree trunk, and the meeting broke up. I walked back into camp with Ham and Don Egriss, but none of us had anything to say. I was wondering how Howard felt about having me be a part of the Revolutionary Committee. I guess this is the first time we have ever done anything together.

When we got back to camp, Edward Heinz was looking for some of us. "Where have you been?" he asked. I told him we were in the meadow. "Well," he said, "didn't you remember that this afternoon we were having the relay races down at the games field?" I *did* forget about them! "My gosh," I said, "I really did forget. I sure am sorry." "You understand, Win, this is the sort of thing I might report you for. What were you, George, Ham, who else? Gogo? What were you all doing up there?" "Gee," I said, "we were just jabbering. I forgot all about the races. I really am sorry." He told me that I was Cabin Leader and he didn't want it to be necessary for me to be sorry another time.

Just before dinner, I saw Paul and told him all that had happened in the meadow, and he said George

67

Meridel had already told him about it and it was pretty strange, the whole thing, and he, for his part, thought Frank Reilley was a one-man nut factory, and it sounded like he was producing nuts. "Does he really expect to get the counselors in The Brig, the cooks, Mr. Warren? Is The Brig big enough?" I said I guessed it was, since that was what they planned.

After dinner I saw Fred Elston, and I said, "We're going to have a revolution tomorrow."

"Who is?"

"We are. Me and Reilley and Ham and Runk and Rivaz and a lot of guys. We're the Revolutionary Committee. We have to put Mr. Warren in The Brig."

Fred Elston was all jittery. "When?"

"Do you want to join the Revolutionary Committee?"

"You bet, man. Thanks. Listen, can Bob Daly join too?"

"Just you. There's already me and Ham from this Cabin. So just you."

"Okay. Swell. Gee, thanks a lot. What do we do now?"

"There'll be a meeting of the Revolutionary Committee at six o'clock tomorrow morning."

He said, "Okay."

"Don't tell anyone about it at all."

"Hey, I'm no fink."

"Not even Bob Daly."

"Hey, I'm no fink."

"What's a fink?"

He shrugged. "Someone who finks. Someone who squeals. But I'm no fink, Weyn. Six o'clock? Hey, be sure and wake me if I don't wake up."

We had the Talent Show all right, but I wasn't thinking much about it, except that I'm sure Paul Indian, playing that Kuhlau sonatina, was the best part. One of the bigger guys, Al Santangelo, has a guitar and plays it pretty well and sings, and he sang a rock-and-roll piece and I guess most of the guys liked that best. Some little kids sang *Blow the Man Down,* it was dreadful, and Ezra Finley, Eddy Hoag and another kid did a little skit about Romeo and Juliet, and there were some other things, but I thought Paul was best. Then, as a surprise, they brought out a movie screen and showed us a couple of cartoons, but they were ancient: *Felix the Cat* and *Popeye,* they moved very jerkily and whole sections seemed to be missing.

Mr. Warren said there would be the weiner roast tomorrow afternoon and we would hike way far down the river more than a mile, where there are a few deep caves for us to explore, and we could have the wiener roast near there. Then we came back to our cabins.

I wrote a short letter to my parents, since they aren't coming here to visit, in which I told them that this is a pretty curious kind of a camp, but it was interesting and I was surviving. I told them how I was captain of the "Capture the Flag" team, and captured the flag myself.

JUNE 5

It was still gray outside, and everyone was there. Frank Reilley, just like a real revolution was going on, posted guards at the head of the path leading into the meadow, so anyone suspicious could be spotted in plenty of time.

First, Frank made it clear to us that he and Stanley Runk were in charge of the revolution, and all orders came down from them.

He pointed out that the nice thing about a revolution and staying out of trouble and sticking together was that it was the kind of game in which we were protected by our own numbers, because who was going to see a hundred kids hurt or even punished seriously? Before they would do that, they would punish the people who ran the camp. Then he said it wouldn't be tough to take over the camp right in the middle of church services, but right after that, during the lunch hour, the visiting begins and relatives would start arriving. We had to have those people leave High Pines without worrying about anything going on up here, because if any relatives learned that the revolution had begun, the revolution would be over. Another problem would be that some of the smaller kids were going out today, and some other kids were coming into the camp. We would have to leave the small kids with no worries about their camp life, Frank said, and so he told us to leave them with the idea that a new game of "Capture the Flag," but with everyone in camp involved, was beginning today (but I sort of changed this order myself, as I will show). Anyhow, giving information out and things like that was part of the propaganda of the revolution, and Frank said we had to have a propaganda committee right away. "It's important work, needing brains," Frank said, and he pointed right at me and went on: "Weyn, I'm making you chairman of the propaganda committee. It carries the rank of lieutenant. You take two guys you can trust and talk to those little twerps and leave them only when they know enough to expect a game to begin this morning, but no more than that."

That was how I became chairman of the propaganda committee and the very first officer appointed by Frank Reilley. You can imagine how surprised I was by that. Ham Pumpernil said he would be on my committee, when I asked him, and Frank told me to make Gogo Burns the second member of my committee.

Next Frank explained that we needed shock troops. The job of the shock troops was to capture the communications points, which were the Administration Building and the storeroom outside, where the public address equipment is kept, and also to take the cooks by surprise and herd them into The Brig. The counselors and Mr. Warren would be captured right at the church services. Jerome Blackridge, Dick Richardson, Manuel Rivaz, John Mason and a couple other big kids were made shock troops, and chief of the shock troops was Jerome Blackridge, with the rank of captain.

Then Pete Bunch asked if all the members of the Revolutionary Committee would get officer rank, and Frank said he believed that would be the case, if not at once, then shortly after the revolution was in charge of

71

High Pines. And then he went back to describing the work of the shock troops. Just before the church services, they were to "capture and hold" the Administration Building (we couldn't help grinning at some of Frank Reilley's words, but he was very serious and got irritated when we grinned, so we didn't grin too much). John Mason was told to give his baboon laugh when the shock troops controlled the Administration Building, and that would be the signal for the church services to be interrupted. Then Frank got very solemn and said, "Now, I said no one is to get hurt, and that's what I mean. You understand? You better! But it's true we may have to look pretty mean about what we're doing. A guy like Taber is a hot-head, we may need to scare him. So don't be surprised if you see old Runk flourishing that sabre of his. That's only another kind of shock troops: fear. You understand? By the time Citizen Warren and the counselors get over being frightened, they're going to be in The Brig and we're going to have ourselves a revolution. That's it. Every guy here whose name I haven't mentioned, you guys will cover the counselors and I'll tell you which guys cover which counselors in a minute." And he went on next to explain that, once the counselors were in The Brig, the biggest kids would be considered counselors by the smaller guys until all visitors had left High Pines. He warned us against there being a leak by any of us or anyone else to the visitors, and looked around with a lot of menace in his face, and his face can be pretty menacing. In fact, Frank Reilley is just odd, and I don't mind admitting he made me shudder a few times because he was talking so strange; like an adult, I mean; like it was a real revolution and a matter of life and death, just like that.

And after saying all these things, he said them again,

assigned kids to cover certain counselors, and then he made Paul Indian what is called "Liaison Officer," which is a little different from me, even though it involves "information." Paul is sort of go-between between officers. Paul scratched his head about being Liaison Officer but didn't object to it, and so that was that. I was surprised by how high Paul's rank was. He was made a captain, just like Jerome Blackridge, but I thought that was pretty good. It sort of makes the revolution look harmless to have me a lieutenant and Paul a captain. At least, I *feel* harmless.

Finally we were sent back to our cabins, pretty nervous. While we were walking back, Ham tickled my ribs and said, "Hey, you must be what they call a born leader. First you were made a Cabin Leader and when these jerks decided Cabin Leaders were no good, they made you a lieutenant even though you were a good Cabin Leader."

But I told Ham, "I wasn't a very good Cabin Leader," and to tell the truth, I wasn't thinking I could make a very good lieutenant, either. Of course, I was happy I had an easy job. All I had to do, as chairman of the propaganda committee, was to talk to a bunch of little kids who probably couldn't comprehend a revolution anyhow, even if it was a real one, and leave them with the idea we were having a good game of Revolutionary "Capture the Flag" while they were going out.

Fred Elston and George Meridel were two of the guys assigned to cover Edward Heinz, by the way. That sure is one job I wouldn't have wanted. George said that, since he is a member of the Revolutionary Committee, later he is going to try to talk Frank Reilley and Stanley Runk into letting him make his Pledge of Allegiance and National Anthem rules good for the whole camp. "Hell," George said, "it might as well be a patriotic revolution." Sometimes I just can't pay much attention to George Meridel, because it hurts.

So I sent Gogo and Ham to hang around the cabins where the smallest kids were, even before breakfast, so they could drop a few words about the game we were going to play. It wasn't called "Revolution," as Frank Reilley had suggested to me at the end of the meeting, because I decided that "revolution" was a kind of dangerous sounding word. I told Ham and Gogo to just sort of mix up the words "war" and "Capture the Flag" so the kids would get the idea there was going to be an enormous game of "Capture the Flag," and after breakfast I went down to their cabins myself and sounded the kids out on what they thought was going to happen after they left, and they felt bad to have to leave right when the whole camp was going to play "Win the War Flag" with real flags. I don't know where they got that name, but I went and told Frank Reilley that the propaganda committee had done its job all right, and that I had forbidden use of the word "revolution" because of its bad sound. Frank was pleased, I guess, because he said, "Smart little bastard," gave me a fishy smile and touched my shoulder, and I think this means he is pleased.

Well, it really happened. It was just minutes after Mr. Warren had begun with the Sunday services that we heard this crazy baboon laugh of John Mason's, and Mr. Warren turned stone white on the platform and said, "Jack, will you see who that was, please?" speaking to Mr. Laudenseller, who is one of the counselors, and Jack Laudenseller got up, but both Frank Reilley and Stanley Runk all at once ran up to the platform and leaped onto it and Frank said "Listen!" And then he got confused, and then he said, "Don't you worry about that sound, Citizen," and Stanley Runk, who looked like he was going to begin giggling, said, "That was just a baboon, see? Don't be scared of one lousy baboon." Mr. Warren said, "You boys sit down at once! Jack, put these two on report. I'll see them directly after the services." "That's right now," said Frank Reilley, "the services are over. Sit down, Laudenseller."

"What are you up to, Reilley?" asked Mr. Laudenseller.

A couple of counselors stood up nervously, looking around.

Stanley Runk suddenly had his knife out, and he was holding one of Mr. Warren's arms behind his back and, standing behind him, he had one of his own arms around Mr. Warren's neck, and Frank said, "Sit down, you guys." They just stood there, and I saw Frank begin to quiver the way he does when he doesn't like the way things are going, he just gets too angry to control himself, and he shouted: "Sit down! Sit down!" The counselors sat down.

"What are you up to, Reilley?" Mr. Laudenseller asked, kind of weakly from where he had sat down.

"Shut up!" shouted Frank.

Mr. Warren looked scared to death and, seeing him look that way, I began to be nearly as scared, too.

Frank took in his breath, and I almost thought he was about to grin. Everybody was still and paying him a lot more attention than they had been paying Mr. Warren.

Frank said, "I represent the High Pines Revolutionary Committee and all officials of High Pines are under arrest. If there is any resistance of any kind, you have my warning: we will act. All counselors are to go directly to The Brig, and I mean without resistance to escorts."

No one moved. The whole scene seemed frozen and for a minute even Frank and Stanley seemed undecided and unable to move. Then Frank seemed to get peeved inside again and continued: "Stanley Runk and I are the leaders of a revolutionary movement which is taking charge of High Pines. Understand this. This is a revolution. The counselors, all of you, will obey me at once. You hear? If we act with force, you'll all suffer— Warren, first. Get them to The Brig!"

There was a big outburst of sounds, but it was just the voices of the counselors trying to change Frank's mind. There was no action against Frank or Stanley, because Stanley was holding that big knife of his up to Mr. Warren's throat. Stanley's face was just as wild and grim as Frank's, even nuttier if anything; I just wasn't sure whether he was serious or not myself, so I could see why the counselors didn't jump up and try to take the knife away from him. Also, some kids had begun to cry.

Frank finally shouted the counselors down, and I believe he could shout down the devil himself, because he seems to go into a positive rage. Then Frank ordered Mr. Warren to tell the counselors to go to The Brig. Stanley Runk brought that knife right up to the skin on Mr. Warren's throat, and Mr. Warren choked out some words about how the counselors had better do as they were told.

What I would like to say about all this, that I cannot quite understand and surely don't know how to explain, is that, especially because I knew it was all a game, I suppose, there was something thrilling about it. It was like a movie, or cops-and-robbers on television. I was excited by seeing Frank Reilley up there. It didn't matter so much about Stanley, and I didn't really like him treating Mr. Warren so badly, but Frank just kind of takes things upon himself and *people obey*. It isn't just that Stanley was threatening Mr. Warren, it's something about Frank Reilley himself. It's the way he talks, I think. Anyhow, I myself was very excited, even more excited than scared, and I noticed that some of the little kids were bawling, so I ran off to the flagpole at the end of the Quad and took down the Bear Flag, ran back and got up on the platform while the counselors and Mr. Warren were being taken away to The Brig. Frank, who was lifting his arms to talk again, looked at me and the Bear Flag and said, "What's that, for Christ's sake?" I was really shaking with excitement by this time, but I told him, kind of hoarsely: "We've captured a flag,". and he got the idea right off, seeing I was trying to comfort the little kids who were scared, and he took the flag from me and held it up and announced: "The first fruits of victory. We got the flag!"

The little kids sort of muffled their tears and the whole batch of kids, who had never, after all, seen Sunday services like this before, just kind of stared at Frank and the Bear Flag.

Frank shouted: "We got the flag!"

A few guys giggled.

Frank waved the flag and grinned and really looked like he was happy to have that flag, and said, "The counselors lose and we win! It's our revolution! It's our flag!" He spoke like having that flag I had brought him was the whole point of everything, and so a few guys clapped their hands. Frank still wasn't satisfied, so he got angry and looked at all the kids and shouted once more: *"We got the flag!"* Then the kids shouted back at him a little, clapped their hands some more, and finally started to cheer. I never saw anything like it, but pretty soon even the littlest kids were cheering like nothing could have made their last day at camp as pleasant as seeing Frank Reilley holding up the Bear Flag during the church services.

While the kids were cheering, some of the shock troops returned and they were sent to the kitchen at the mess hall to get the cooks to The Brig, and then Frank called Paul up to the platform: "Captain Indian!"

Paul went up and stood beside us, and Frank lifted his hands until all the kids were quiet: "Paul here is going to go over to the mess hall in a couple minutes, and in celebration of a bunch of new kids coming in and some of you smaller kids going out today, we're going to empty the place of everything that's good. You understand? Whatever you want today, it's yours. Ice cream, cookies, cake, Kool-aid, whatever you want."

So that made the kids clap their hands some more, and Frank talked to them a few more minutes, wanting to be sure the cooks were gone, I guess, and he joked and made the kids laugh, and I was amazed to see him, because I have to admit he was entertaining those kids a lot more than Mr. Warren could. I could see the kids really did understand that the whole thing was a game, however strange, and what's more, I could see that, even though they didn't have much to do with it, they were enjoying the game; and this is because, as I could see, they *liked* Frank. It was like he was one of them, and Mr. Warren never had been. Anyhow, pretty soon Frank sent the smallest kids over with Paul and a couple of guys to raid the kitchen. It was a pretty happy-looking revolution, we nearly seemed to have liberated those kids.

The kids who were left were those who were staying, either medium-aged kids or big guys, and Frank became very serious with them, but I could see even when he tried to be solemn that he himself was excited and nervous. I think he was happy, as happy as the small kids going over to eat ice cream, but anyhow he spoke solemnly: "You have just been a part of a bloodless coup"—incidentally Frank may be a straight-A student but he said *coop*, like in *chicken coop,* and the word is really pronounced *koo,* but to go on: "I am General Frank Reilley. My partner is General Stanley Runk. If you find these titles funny, fine, we have nothing against laughter. If you find them too funny, though, I'll tell you this: we mean to maintain order in this revolution, and when I say we mean to maintain it, you believe it. Those kids on their way to the mess hall, they're having more fun right now than they were fifteen minutes ago. Isn't that right? Well, that's all this revolution is about: fun. We're going to have some fun. Citizen Warren's sermons are over for the duration, however short that is. For all who cooperate with the revolution, the rewards will be fun, fun like you may have dreamed of having but never had the chance to have. I mean, things are going to *happen* up here. But for right now, just remember that the revolution is in charge of High Pines, and I and Runk are in charge of the revolution. You treat us as counselors for the rest of the day, you hear me? We are your counselors when visitors start popping in, which is going to be real soon, and no matter what happens, you keep quiet about the revolution. If you have a visitor, you'll be watched. You let one word out, just one, and your relatives wind up in The Brig, and you wind up in the river, so help me. Understood? Any action taken against us will be considered counterrevolutionary, and punishment will be severe. Listen, though, I'm not looking for any of you to be dumb enough to try to make trouble for all the rest of us, because that would be just bull-headed rottenness, one guy trying to take away everyone else's fun. Be patient, sit tight and for a day or so you're going to learn what fun is, you're going to learn *how* to have fun. Okay? After that, it's up to you; you can go back to your God-damned butterflies. That's all for now. Sit tight and don't get yourselves or anyone else in trouble. Again, soon visitors will be here. I am your counselor. Runk is your counselor, but don't press him," and some of the guys laughed edgily at this, "and any big guy near you is a counselor. You get the idea. If you have questions, direct them to me or to Runk or to Jerry Blackridge. You are forbidden to say a word about the revolution, even to use the word *revolution*, and if you have complaints and can't find myself, Runk or Blackridge, take them to Paul Indian. He's Liaison Officer. Rivaz, come up here. Rivaz is in charge here till I get back. Members of the Revolutionary Committee will report at once to the Administration Building," and that is about the gist of the first speech of the revolution, and I will just say it shook not just me, but the whole camp. The guys really began to chatter when we walked from the Quad to the Administration Building.

I have to remark, though, that it seemed like a very peaceful revolution so far. It even seemed well planned, although there had been only the one meeting in the morning. But, except for the small kids crying a little, there was no breaking down or anything like that. The one thing that did make me uncomfortable, though, is that Don Egriss just sat still from the beginning right on through the whole "coup." He just sat there, hardly even watching, dead-faced, maybe even sad-looking, though I couldn't see his face much and was too excited myself to watch it much. He was still sitting there like that when we walked out of the Quad.

Boy, that was a nervous meeting. Paul came in late and said, "At least the cooks left lunch for us." Gogo Burns asked, "What are we having?" Frank got irritated and said, "Shut up, you guys, we got business. We just got a few minutes," he was wiping sweat off his forehead, "that bus will be here any time. The little kids have to be ready to go, we have to get the new kids in and placed in cabins. Then visitors will be streaming in. Ham Pumpernil!" Ham stepped forward. "You," said Frank, "Fred Elston tells me you know about radio operation, electronics, that sort of stuff." Ham said, "I know a little." So Frank went on, "You're Communications Officer. It carries the rank of lieutenant. I want the public address system set up. You're in charge of equipment and the storeroom," and he tossed Ham some keys, "all right?"

Next, Frank startled us by saying he had to let Mr. Warren out of The Brig. It seemed he figured too many parents might know Mr. Warren personally, so they would have to be able to see him. But Frank said he would be under close guard all the while he was out, and as soon as the visitors were gone he'd go straight back to The Brig. I felt sorry for Mr. Warren, but I was sure there was nothing I could do about it. Then Frank pointed out that, so long as we had visitors, Cabin Leaders were still Cabin Leaders. Then Frank made my brother Howard head of a committee to welcome the new kids and get them to their cabins, which didn't please Howard, but it was an order. Then Frank appointed guys to make a list of lunch-serving details.

Ham said, "Where shall I set up the public address system?"

"I want to know how many speakers we have, and how much cord," Frank told him, "because I think we got quite a lot of equipment. I definitely want a speaker up in the Quad, so get going on that, and report to me about whatever else we have. Jerry Blackridge has been promoted to Chief of the Revolutionary Police, with the rank of colonel, so when he talks, you guys listen. You listen! He's in charge at The Brig, and being with the Revolutionary Police is going to be important work around this place, so pass the word, because I want dependable guys to volunteer for this duty." Frank took a minute to think, and he sighed and was really beginning to look less fidgety and I could tell he was still excited and happy. He was just plain having a good time. Frank couldn't think of more to say, and so he said, "Any questions? If not, move out!" You'd have thought it was a real revolution in Vietnam or something. Stanley Runk, who had been gaping around through all this talk, suddenly said, "Move out!" after Frank had said it, as if someone might have forgotten he had the rank to say so. So we moved out.

I went to help Ham get the equipment out of the storeroom, saying, "Allow me to help you, Lieutenant Pumpernil," and he saying, "My great thanks, Lieutenant Weyn." There were five speakers, in all, which surprised us, so Ham went to find Frank and ask him where to string them up. I went back to my cabin to be a Cabin Leader.

After a time, Communications Officer Pumpernil rang the lunch bell. I couldn't help feeling shocked to see Mr. Warren walking to the mess hall, but of course he had Stanley Runk on one side of him, Frank Reilley on the other, with both Jerome Blackridge and Dick Richardson behind, and he also knew, as I learned later, that if he made any trouble while he was out, it might be taken out on one of the counselors in The Brig. I looked at Mr. Warren, but it embarrassed me to see how unconfident he looked, so I didn't look at him again.

There were quite a few grown-ups walking around, mostly with this kid or that kid, and they came up to eat at the mess hall, too. I guess there were nearly thirty visitors in all.

During lunch, Mr. Warren himself got up and said, "A big wiener roast is scheduled for this afternoon, a distance down our river, and we think your boys will all want to be in on it, and if they do, they should plan to be right here at the mess hall no later than one-thirty. We'll start from here. If there are any boys who would rather skip the wiener roast and spend a little more time with their folks, they are free to do so; just leave your names with your counselors. However, visiting hours end not long after we'll get started, anyhow, and I hope all the boys will be coming on the outing with us." Mr. Warren said a few more words without much enthusiasm and then sat down, and I guess it would have been pretty hard to tell there was a revolution going on around him, or that Frank Reilley had probably told him exactly what to say.

The whole new bunch of kids, mostly just a couple years younger than me, or thereabouts, have the cabins the smallest kids were using, and I guess they were pretty bewildered for a while, or maybe they were interested enough in just getting to High Pines so that they didn't have time to wonder why they were herded to their cabins so quickly, and then to the mess hall. At lunch, Ham whispered to me, "Boy, I sure won't go on any wiener roast this afternoon. Frank says he wants all five of those speakers put up." "Where?" I asked him. "Well, I already got one up in the Quad, and I got to put another here at the mess hall, then one down by the new kids' cabins, one up by our cabins and the other one way down the river, so it serves one of the swimming areas and the meadow." "Boy, that will take you all day. Have you got enough wire?" "Oh, said Ham, "I got a thousand miles of cord, but it will take me all day, all right. It's dumb. By the time I get all those things put up, the whole revolution will be over. I'll be the only one left fighting it."

JUNE 6

It's early in the morning and I'll go on about yesterday, because there was too much to write last night and I was too tired to keep it up.

Well, all the visitors left and I guess no one said anything to them about the revolution. After they went, there was the meeting at the mess hall. I went over early and watched while Ham and Taylor Walk were fixing the loudspeaker to the outer rafter of the mess hall. It was attached to a long black wire that disappeared in the trees alongside the path leading down to the river and over to the Quad, and Ham was putting it up with a couple of nails, standing perched on a ladder which Taylor was holding steady. Ham was still up on that ladder, his head just about sticking into the big loudspeaker, when suddenly Frank Reilley's voice came spitting out of it, sounding like his lungs were made of metal:

"This is General Reilley speaking. This is General Reilley speaking," and Ham nearly fell off the ladder; he hurried down it like he thought General Reilley was chasing him, and he was on the ground even before General Reilley could go on speaking. "This is an important announcement. All visitors have left High Pines. The revolution thanks you for your cooperation. High Pines is now in absolute control of our revolutionary forces. There will be a meeting at the mess hall at two sharp, if you haven't heard about it already, so start moving. There will be a short meeting of the Revolutionary Committee beginning at one-forty-five, at the Administration Building." "What about the wiener roast?" some guy nearby asked, so I missed something Frank had said, but heard him go on: "Colonel Blackridge is in charge of the Revolutionary Police, and it is his job to keep order here so long as the revolution lasts. Everyone at High Pines is considered to be a member of the Revolutionary Militia, and is subject to orders from myself, General Runk or Colonel Blackridge. No one will leave camp for any purpose, and if anyone tries, he will be dealt with. Any action against the revolution, such as trying to leave camp, will be classified as counterrevolutionary, and counterrevolution means trouble. Lieutenant Winston Weyn," he spoke my name and I felt like I must have broken some revolutionary rule already and got scared, "Lieutenant Weyn will report at once to General Reilley, that's me, at the Administration Building. Well," he seemed to think for a time, "that's all for now," and after another pause Frank said, "Goodbye, then," like he had been on a telephone, and then the humming sound of the loudspeaker seemed to burn out and everyone stood around staring at it.

I beat it straight over to the Administration Building, thinking I was probably on my way to The Brig for the rest of the whole game, but it turned out Frank just wanted to see me because I am chairman of the propaganda committee.

"Win," said Frank (and this was the very first time he called me by my first name, that I can recollect), "we still have a problem. The whole new group of kids have been briefed by Indian, but they're pretty shaken up, maybe, and I'm making it your job to let them know fully how things stand with the revolution. I'm counting on you to make them cooperate with us, and not just stay on the sidelines watching. Try to pick out those guys who are really interested in the revolution and maybe have some guts. Get names, and more than anything, be sure and let me know the names of any who might make trouble for us. You understand?"

I said, "Okay."

He said, "Win, we have to keep things in order around here, you can see that. Revolution is made out of disorder, but even though we mean to have some fun, the object of even this kind of revolution has to be some degree of order. That's right, isn't it?"

"Sure," I said, supposing it must be true. After all he gets plenty of A's and is a lot older than I am.

"Then say, *yes sir,*" he told me.

I nodded and said, "Yes, sir."

"That's all, Lieutenant," he said, going back to being my superior officer.

I said, "Yes, sir," and for some reason or other I saluted him, which made him give me one of those great smiles of his and he even saluted me back.

"Say," I said, "sir, now that things are settling down a little, I'd like to have a couple more guys on the propaganda committee."

"Why?"

"Now that Ham is Communications Officer, I only have Gogo, and he's kind of small, like me. Could I have Bob McCarthy and maybe Don Egriss on the propaganda committee?"

"Egriss?" Frank gave me a couple of suspicious glances and went on, "He's a doubtful character, isn't he?"

"Oh," I said, "Don's just doubtful because he's intelligent."

So after a minute Frank made another piece of a grin, saying, "Yeah, okay. If Egriss is willing to be on your committee, take him."

"Thank you, sir." I saluted, backing out of the Presence.

He didn't smile back at me, either. This time he just saluted, and pretty smartly.

So I went straight to the cabin and found Bob McCarthy there, reading from my Bible, and I told him he had been appointed to my propaganda committee. He said, "I guess I'd get The Brig if I refused." I said, "Go ahead and refuse, then. I got permission to ask Don Egriss to be on my committee, too." Bob asked, "Is he joining your committee?" I had to admit I didn't know, but I said that at least I had permission to ask Don. So Bob McCarthy thought about it and finally agreed to go with me down to the mess hall to see if Don was there.

We found Don sipping Kool-aid through a straw, sitting on a bench and all slouched over his glass. I sat down beside him and said, "Don, will you do me a favor?" He didn't look over, he just kept his mouth around his straw and muttered, "Uh uh." I asked him again, and he said nothing at all except to suck up Kool-aid, so I said, "Join my propaganda committee, Don, will you?" That made him sit up anyhow, although he moved very slowly. He turned and looked at me and I could see he was asking me if I was serious. Then he said, "Beat it, Lieutenant." He meant it. So I went with Bob McCarthy and got Gogo Burns and we headed down to the cabins where the new guys stay.

We talked to the new kids awhile and explained how Frank had made this revolution and how it was only supposed to last a short while. A lot of them were pretty confused and some of them really didn't like the revolution at all, but they all agreed they wouldn't do anything against the revolution, and that was the main point.

We went to the mess hall where the rest of the guys were already having their meeting. Stanley Runk was up on the side platform there, telling all the kids that the revolution would maybe be short, but it was going to be a gay one, sports, and so I went to tell Frank Reilley that everything went off okay with the new kids, but that Don Egriss didn't care to join my committee. Frank shrugged and studied the list of names I gave him of the kids who might be willing to join the revolution and those who seemed a little scared about it. I went back and sat down at my table and looked around the mess hall to see if things had changed much. I guess they hadn't, except it was Stanley Runk up there doing the talking instead of Mr. Warren, and so it was kind of wild talk.

"Hey, Runk," yelled someone whose voice was familiar, though I couldn't see his face.

"*General* Runk, Shorty," shouted Stanley, clapping his hands and doing a little dance on the table on to which he had jumped.

"Hey, General Runk," yelled the guy, "is there any rule about how much we have to smoke, drink, swear and piss in the river?"

"What's the matter?" shouted Stanley back at the guy. "You got tight kidneys or something? I want this place contaminated!"

A lot of guys were laughing and Frank Reilley stood up and put his arm around Stanley and put his other hand up for quiet. "Okay," said Frank, "don't lose control right in the mess hall, what do you say? You guys can sure as hell see we've got nothing against a little enjoyment, only we still got work to do before we open up on the fun. For example, we have another prisoner to capture around four o'clock, when Miss Newman comes."

"Hey!" said Stanley. "I'll assign twenty guys to cover Nurse Newman. Volunteers! Volunteers!"

Laughter.

"Don't laugh," cried Stanley. "That woman is heavy!"

More laughter.

"Okay," Frank put his hands high again, "only it isn't as easy as it sounds. The revolution isn't over until we're really in charge here, and we got work. Think!" Frank's strange grin all at once vanished and there he was standing with his hands up and a big scowl on his face, and he looked like he was about to hypnotize everyone, and maybe that's what he did, because everything suddenly went quiet. "Think!" he said again, and slowly he let his hands come down. "Miss Newman's cabin isn't here. It's at Low Pines, it's at the girls' camp. Think, little revolutionaries, think. She'll be expected to return to Low Pines. She won't return. Think." Gradually he let his shuddery smile come back on to his face and, even if it is a crazy smile, it almost makes Frank kind of handsome, though that isn't quite the word I want. "That's right. The revolution is a long way from being over. Now, all Stan the Punk has said about having a good time, let me tell you: that goes! Fun is in! You're going to have a good time, beginning with a party right here in this mess hall, but I mean a party, a real party, not wieners and marshmallows. A party! Liquor, girls, everything."

"Girls!" a big cry went up all over the mess hall and a lot of guys began to laugh and clap their hands and scream, "Girls!"

"Sure," Frank asked for quiet again. "Sure, girls. Because the revolution has got to carry over into the girls' camp, into Low Pines, and that's the purpose of this meeting. This revolution isn't over until we're in charge, and we can't be in charge of one camp without being in charge of both of them. The revolution's next objective: Low Pines."

A lot more shouts went up, and most of them were guys saying they wanted to volunteer for the war against the girls' camp.

"Now listen to me," Frank scowled and seemed very angry all at once, "Listen! Listen! Listen!" The guys listened. "Not everyone can participate in the assault on the girls' camp. I'll take about thirty, maybe thirty-five guys. Well now, Egriss, you look gloomy. You need exercise. You want to march on the girls' camp with us?" I couldn't see Don very well, but I think he just sneered at Frank. "No?" Frank went on. "Fine. Then I'm ordering you to take charge of the kitchen, Egriss, and don't think an order from me doesn't mean anything right now. You take four or five guys you think can cook and get dinner started. If they argue with you, tell them you're a corporal." Laughter and hooting and, it was strange, with all that laughter, even Don had to look up and grin after a bit, but I don't think he liked what Frank said. Then Frank read off a big long list of names, including my own and Ham's, and including Oly Anderson and Mike Derr and Sam Gabrenya (all new guys who just arrived yesterday) and including Pete Bunch, Fred Elston, Bob Daly, Frank Divordich, Howard, Gogo, George Meridel, Manuel Rivaz—too many guys to name them all, but I knew most of them. Frank said that a "rear guard" would head over toward Low Pines at once, through the woods, and that the main force of guys would head out after Miss Newman had come to be captured.

So when Miss Newman came, it all went very

smoothly. She just walked into the Administration Building and Frank said, "Hello, Miss Newman. You're under arrest," and she laughed at that, but then Frank got on one side of her and Stanley on the other and they each took an arm and she asked them, "What are you boys doing?" Frank said, "You're the nurse, aren't you?" She nodded and said, "Is someone hurt?" Stanley said, "You're a morbid old lady." Miss Newman asked Stanley what he meant by that and Stanley told her that she was a nurse and so she should know about morbid conditions and things like that, and she turned to Frank and said, "Let me go! What are you doing? Where are you taking me?" Frank said, "You happen to be a nurse, don't you?" And the whole conversation repeated itself until finally they had talked her right into a cabin, where she was left under guard; and I guess she still didn't know what was happening even after she was a prisoner. This is what Stanley Runk told me (when he could stop laughing about it) while we were driving over to Low Pines.

There was something worse about being in the station wagon (Mr. Warren's station wagon, and we also had Miss Newman's car), with Stanley Runk driving, than anything that had happened so far. In the first place, we had left High Pines, and there was something about leaving the camp which made the situation more like real warfare or something. In the second place, I don't know what it is, but not being on my feet and being transported somewhere on wheels, it made me feel strange, even a little sick.

We went into the girls' camp from two different directions, and my group headed straight for the Administration Building. It was very simple. We walked in, a woman looked up at us, and her face went blank. She didn't seem able to figure out anything at all to explain our presence. Stanley was standing between the woman and the telephone on the wall and he asked her, "Where's The Brig?" "The what?" asked the woman, and she said, "What are you doing, who are you, get out of here, do you want me to call for help, are you from High Pines?"—a thousand or so little questions just poured out of her mouth and kept pouring until Stanley, who seemed confused for awhile, said, "Shut up, Skinny. You're under arrest." *"Arrest!"* screeched that woman (she was Mrs. Knute), "why, you aren't police!" "No, but at least I'm General Runk, girlie, you just call me Punk, and this is a revolution. Where is The Brig in this camp?" "What are you talking about? You're crazy, you get out of here!" And so Stanley pulled out that hunting knife of his and said, "Where's The Brig?" "What do you mean," she asked, "the detention room?" "Sure, sure," said the General, "where is it?" "It's none of your business," said the woman, and she might have said more but Stanley began to wiggle his knife around in the air a little and chuckled just a little and Mrs. Knute suddenly shut her mouth. She got up and led us to the detention room, a smaller cabin than our own Brig, and Stanley locked Mrs. Knute up in there.

Leaving a guard behind, we moved on, girls beginning to appear here and there in gym shorts, squealing and gasping and giggling and gaping and screaming and running and standing and staring stupidly. We saw Frank's squad of guys down the way and they had four women in tow, maybe as old as twenty or even older on the average, one of them being very beautiful. Stanley gave Frank the keys to the detention room and Frank sent some guys to lock up the women, who were Low Pines counselors, and then I heard Fred Elston's rear guard come whooping down the hill, gobbling like terrified turkeys, and I suppose they were rounding up the girls down by the river like they were dogs and the girls were sheep; anyhow, that is about all I saw and heard of the campaign, myself, because I was one of the guys sent over to guard the detention room.

I know it took quite a while to take over the camp, though; maybe more than two hours, and Frank told me himself he really had to work hard to "pacify" all the girls. A lot of them thought it was a real revolution and they wouldn't do anything but bawl for a half hour or so, and Jerome Blackridge, I was told, slapped a couple of girls around because of this, because they were hysterical; and I guess that is the sort of job Blackridge would like. But otherwise it was pretty much the same as at the boys' camp, which surprised me very much. Once they had got all the counselors and cooks to the detention room, there was a big conference—with guards from High Pines standing all around, of course—and Frank spoke to the girls for quite a while. Very quickly he had Ham set up a microphone for him, and Ham said Frank spoke like he had really come to liberate Low Pines from some tyrants, and that Frank was quick to find cooperative girls (a girl named Susan Langer has been made a colonel and put in charge at Low Pines, although there has always to be a couple of squads from High Pines over there, just to make sure things keep running like Frank wants them to run). Ham said Frank even brought God into his speech, and that it was an even wilder speech than Ham had heard him make at High Pines, and that although Frank had used the word "fun" in his speech as being the purpose of the revolution, he made the word sound different than he had made it sound with the boys. Ham said it sounded more pretty, more innocent or something, more like a children's party which would have its beginning and its end. So even though the girls are probably not as cooperative as the boys, on the whole, they are apparently "pacified" over there, and are being kept in line. Frank told me that, even with all the work it took, things had gone off easier at Low Pines than he had expected, and that he doesn't believe any girls will make trouble for the revolution. But I think girls are different from boys, and even though Frank is such a good talker and talked to them so long, I'll still be surprised if the girls don't stop the revolution by dinnertime today (which is all right with me because, after all, it has got to end pretty soon or we'll all be in bad trouble). Speaking of dinner, Frank did *one* good thing at Low Pines, anyhow: he got Susan Langer to agree to appoint squads of girls to help do the cooking at High Pines, and I think that even pleased Don Egriss. Which reminds me that it is breakfast time right now, and I probably have missed it.

Just to finish about yesterday, then: last night, Miss Newman was sent back to the girls' camp to be put in the detention room there, and us guys who had been in on the Low Pines campaign had a late dinner, which didn't matter much because Don Egriss' kitchen squad couldn't even cook beans without them coming out like little piles of tar and gravel.

I noticed after dinner that a number of guys were smoking, such as General Runk the Punk, Jerome Blackridge and Manuel Rivaz, and I wondered where they got cigarettes, and suppose they must have had them all along.

After dinner, too, there was a little griping among some guys because everything was pretty silent and there was no fun, like Frank and Stanley had said there would be, but Frank had me pass around the word that the fun was going to begin though the revolution was still going on. That's what he said. And it kind of depressed me; it certainly takes a long time to make one little revolution. Of course, it has been an exciting day, even scary. I know the revolution is bad, in a way, and I am sure Don Egriss is right to stay out of it, and I know I am a little scared about everything. But maybe it is because I am a lieutenant, or chairman of the propaganda committee, or maybe it's something else; I only know that, even while I think the revolution had better be called off soon, yesterday was surely the most exciting day of my life.

Ham said that Don Egriss told him that Mr. Warren has said that if he and the counselors are freed right away, only the few guys responsible for the revolution, at the very top, would be in trouble. I don't even know if this includes me or not, but I am afraid it might, since I am an officer. Of course, I don't know if Mr. Warren really said that or not.

JUNE 6

I am not going to write much because I am very tired. I am also still scared and I suppose I am still excited, but I am disgusted, too. To begin with, those girls can't cook better than the boys. Not only that, there will be a supply problem if they go on ruining stuff and throwing away stuff like those girls did today. They wasted big vats full of food and so just had to throw it away. Of course, there is plenty of food and stuff, a whole refrigerator-vault full, and powdered milk, and Kool-aid and plenty of everything I suppose, but Mr. Warren is going to be plenty mad about how much we have wasted when the revolution is over. Lunch and dinner were both late, and should have been called off entirely, considering how they tasted.

Today a Supreme Revolutionary Committee was formed, with some girls on it, but I'm not a member. The members of the Supreme Revolutionary Committee are Frank Reilley, Stanley Runk, Jerome Blackridge, Manuel Rivaz, Paul Indian, Susan Langer, Edna Kay, Jean Laughlin and Bernice Royer. Everyone on the Supreme Revolutionary Committee has to be at least a captain. Frank and Stanley are generals, of course, and Blackridge and Susan Langer are colonels. Manuel Rivaz and Edna Kay are majors, and the rest are captains. Frank had me announce all these ranks over the public-address system, it somehow being a part of "propaganda," and I also announced that all authority in High Pines and Low Pines would be maintained by the Supreme Revolutionary Committee.

And, except for one terrible thing, that is about all that happened all day today. It was Frank Divordich, of all people, who got tired of the revolution and said the cooking was lousy, and so he went to his cabin and got his things together and just started to walk right out of the camp. I don't know where he thought he was going, maybe he meant to walk all the way home, but he was stopped by a guard toward the front of the camp and was taken to Colonel Blackridge. And Blackridge said that Divordich was "subject to counter-revolutionary punishment"—this is what Divordich told me afterward. "Why did you try to leave camp?" asked Blackridge. Divordich said he only wanted to go home, since he didn't like the camp any more. "Didn't you know there are rules against leaving High Pines?" "Sure," said Frank, but he pointed out that he was tired of the whole game. "You're tired of the game," said Blackridge, "so the thing to do is to run out and tell the first person you meet what a bad game it is. Isn't that right?" Divordich said he hadn't meant to say anything to anyone. "No," said Blackridge, "you just meant to walk a couple of hundred miles without talking to anyone, and you didn't even mean to talk to your folks at home." Blackridge said that Divordich was a traitor to the revolution, and so without even asking anyone about it, he took Divordich up to the meadow and tied him to a tree and he actually beat Divordich on the back with his belt. Hard! Divordich cried out so loud that they gagged him, but he got beaten ten to fifteen times, he says.

Poor Divordich was plenty mad when he came back

to the cabin and he wouldn't even tell anyone what. happened, but late tonight he told me about it, because he was crying and I heard him. Tomorrow I'm going to tell Don Egriss what happened. This is a terrible thing. Shameful. Jerome Blackridge had no right even to tie Divordich to a tree, much less to hit him.

I looked at Divordich's back and it has got big marks on it, all right, so I was reminded of how my father beat me with a belt the last time. I told Divordich all I know on the subject of pain, and how if he concentrated deeply he wouldn't feel the pain at all, but Divordich didn't understand a bit of it, he just cried angrily, "It hurts," and finally went to sleep. I guess it still hurts him and I'm both mad and scared about this. And Frank said no one was going to get hurt. It is time we stopped this whole game.

JUNE 7

The very first thing this morning, there was a message over the loudspeakers. I had just come up to the mess hall and almost everyone was there to hear General Stanley the Punk announce:

"Yesterday an important rule was broken in this camp. God damn it, we told you early enough that the punishment for counterrevolutionaries wasn't part of the fun we got planned for High Pines. We're giving the little runt another chance, we didn't even stick the lout in The Brig. Now, unless you want to get yourself hurt, just don't break any rules around here. Nobody leaves this camp in any direction, for any reason, without permission. Which you ain't likely to get." In a minute Stanley said more cheerfully, "This has been the happy General, Stanley L. Runk, the Punk himself, broadcasting straight from the Administration Building. Cheerio! You slobs can finish your breakfast now."

I went and sat beside Don Egriss and told him what Frank Divordich had told me, and how he had big marks on his back. Don just shook his head and said, "The butterflies are gone, kid. What did you expect?" I was surprised by that and said, "Don't you care?" He looked at me madly and said, "Is caring fun, kid?" So I left his table, noticing that Al Santangelo was sitting right across from Don and seemed to be watching us kind of strangely and he heard what I said, I guess, so I began to worry about that, thinking they might begin to watch me and maybe even charge me with being a counterrevolutionary.

It was a gloomy day and I had a lot of time and so I took my book on political philosophers and began to read from it, but it is very difficult, certainly more difficult than Herodotus, and I guess you need a lot of knowledge just to understand this stuff. So what I am doing is trying to pick out those places which aren't too hard, which I can understand. The book has writings in it by Thomas Jefferson, Henry David Thoreau, John Stuart Mill, John Locke, Adam Smith and Karl Marx, though not in that order. One thing I noticed about the book, and this interested me very much because I noticed before that history has had something to do with money and the value of things, is that whenever these philosophers seem to write about liberty and stuff, they right away begin to talk about money and labor and commodities (things for sale). So maybe I was on the right track. But in a way, reading about prices and things is very boring, and anyhow I can't understand a great deal of it.

Today, George Meridel passed around a petition asking that his rules to make everyone say the Pledge of Allegiance and sing the National Anthem every morning be put into effect right away at both High Pines and Low Pines, but Frank found out he was passing out a petition and blew his top. He said petitions were counterrevolutionary, and that scared Meridel nearly out of his one pair of shorts (I would guess). He looked about as sickening as a cocker spaniel with a guilt complex or something, and this was right in public, and he said, "I didn't know it was counterrevolutionary, sir." So Frank told him if he had any requests, he should make them directly to the

Supreme Revolutionary Committee at the Administration Building. George saluted. The way George saluted made me feel kind of funny; all at once his hand snapped up to his forehead, and his hand seemed to have taken its clothes off and was a girl and I shouldn't have been looking—I don't know how to explain it. Except to say that I think it is really his brain that is naked.

JUNE 8

That smelly rat, George Meridel, came up behind me last night and grabbed my diary right out of my hands right while I was writing about his naked brain, and ran off into the dark. I couldn't catch him and I was mad as I could be. He went off by himself some place, and I just hope he enjoyed the parts about himself.

But what did he do? Here's what: he went and gave my diary to Frank Reilley and reported to Frank that I was reading stuff by Karl Marx. That's what he did. And Frank sent for me and gave it back—right after giving me something else first, which was a real dressing down. But all this really backfired on George, though, because the result of the dressing down is that Frank asked me to join the Supreme Revolutionary Committee, as a captain. Boy, I'll bet that burned up old Meridel, when he heard that.

I couldn't understand the offer because, after all, I haven't written only good things about the revolution and even about Frank, and Frank himself told me that the things I was writing in this diary were counterrevolutionary, and it seemed strange to be raised in rank right after being counterrevolutionary; especially seeing as Frank Divordich got beaten with a belt on the same charge.

Well, there are certain advantages to being on the Supreme Revolutionary Committee (the S.R.C., they call it), such as being able to know what's going on from hour to hour, which is kind of a privilege these days. Anyhow I am now Captain Weyn, and still chairman of the propaganda committee, and I must admit that I think it was kind of Frank Reilley to treat me pretty well considering that I have written some peculiar things about him in here, which surely he must have seen.

I was thinking that the first thing I should do as a member of the S.R.C. would be to denounce George Meridel as counterrevolutionary, but I couldn't think of anything to denounce him for, except his petition, and Frank Reilley had already taken care of that. I could have pointed out that Meridel stole an officer's private papers, but I didn't want to call any more attention to my diary, so there was nothing I could do.

Frank called a meeting early this afternoon, at the Low Pines Administration Building, and he asked me to bring my Bible, which I did, and I drove out with him and Manuel Rivaz. Stanley and Blackridge and Paul were already there. While we were driving, Frank said, "Tonight we're going to have a party, Win. I know this is late notice, but then the party is late in getting under way. As soon as we get back to High Pines, I want you to get your propaganda committee busy spreading the word. Dancing, music, liquor, everything. At the High Pines mess hall. The girls that want to come will come, and Susie thinks that might mean as many as forty, maybe even more, so it'll be a real ball." I asked Frank why we might need liquor. Manuel Rivaz laughed and said, "Maybe you don't need it, boy. Maybe you, you're like me, huh? Me, I was born at a thirty-degree angle, I been tipsy ever since." Frank wasn't in a laughing mood, which on the whole is good for Frank, and he said, "I promised the guys fun and I mean to provide it. I don't break promises, Win—you'll learn that." And he told me the party was to begin at seven-thirty and everyone was invited.

The S.R.C. meeting was pretty much about the party tonight and I met a kind of pretty girl before the meeting, named Evelyn Wright, who is chairman of propaganda at Low Pines (but Frank let her know she was under me in the propaganda department). Evelyn, who is a couple of months older than I am, had the job of publicizing our party at the girls' camp. I don't think she likes me at all, for some reason, but I don't think she is so smart, either. Anyhow, she isn't a member of the S.R.C.

Also, at the meeting, Frank said the revolution is still going on, it isn't even over yet. This really flabbergasted me and I couldn't think what else had to be done, but Frank Reilley put it this way:

"Nothing stands still. Things are either growing or decaying, that's all I learned in biology. Things are either going in one direction or another, that's all I learned in physics. People are either pushing to the left or to the right, that's all I learned in history. The only thing I learned in school is that nothing stands still, and when something stops getting bigger, it starts getting smaller. If the revolution is done growing, the revolution has collapsed, and this is my revolution, and it's not going to collapse until I'm finished with it. And I won't be finished with it till I've kept my promises about having plenty of fun. When this revolution ends, I want every girl and boy in on it to be *sorry* it's over. You all better understand that right now. Jerry Blackridge has made an important suggestion. He says we should all take loyalty oaths, to swear loyalty to the revolution for so long as it lasts. Then we have to agree that anyone breaking that oath gets a really fitting punishment."

We discussed that idea of Blackridge's for a time and I didn't like it. For example, if I had sworn loyalty to the revolution a couple of days ago, I wouldn't have had any right to quit if someone got beaten, even if it was Paul or Ham or Don Egriss instead of Frank Divordich. Blackridge said that if he had not beaten Frank Divordich, there was no telling how many guys might have tried to walk out. Frank said he agreed that something had to be done with counterrevolutionaries, but that it was up to the S.R.C. and not Blackridge by himself to decide what to do with them.

In the end, we took a vote and it was six to four in favor of having a loyalty oath, with a "fitting punishment" for whoever broke the oath. I, Paul, Bernice Royer and Edna Kay were the four to vote against the oath. Frank, Stanley, Jerome Blackridge, Manuel Rivaz, Susan Langer and Jean Laughlin voted for the oath. Of course, everyone knows that Jean Laughlin has a crush on Manuel Rivaz and she would vote however he voted, even though she knows he likes this other girl, named May. Then it turned out Blackridge had written out the oath already and so we all had to say it right on the spot, with one hand on my Bible: "I swear loyalty to the High Pines and Low Pines revolution, and to the leaders, and will never betray it, so help me God." We all took that oath, although I admit that, being an atheist, I wasn't sure whether I was supposed to feel bound by it or not. I guess atheists are just supposed to keep their word all the time, since they have no God to swear to.

And that was the end of the meeting, except for short reports on the boys' camp (from Frank) and the girls' camp (from Susan, who made it sound like the girls were having more fun than the boys, because they had already started a schedule of games and parties at the girls' camp, whereas the boys were still waiting for some fun), and both Frank and Susan seemed to think both camps were "pacified" and they didn't expect any bad trouble to arise. It was agreed that cars would arrive to begin taking girls to the party tonight a little after seven o'clock. Then the S.R.C. meeting was adjourned.

I got permission from Frank to enlarge my propaganda committee, and now the whole committee stays at my cabin, Number Nine, which is known as *H.Q., Propaganda,* and I have a little desk there and the mimeograph machine from the Administration Building, and the members of my committee are now as follows: Ham Pumpernil, Bob McCarthy, Frank Divordich (who isn't exactly brainy, but we have been getting along better since he got beaten and I feel kind of sorry for him), Gogo Burns, Taylor Walk and Sam Gabrenya. Ham is still a lieutenant and Communications Officer, but Frank decided that communications was a proper part of propaganda, and so I have a lieutenant on my "staff." Ham, when he heard I was a captain, said, "What did I tell you? You're a born leader. You'll be General before it's over and then what will you do?" "Free the girls," I said, which everyone took as a joke. This is a good committee I have now, because we all get along quite well.

Publicizing a party is easy, especially when you have a "captive audience." I wrote up about ten different announcements and made four of them myself and let the other guys make the rest of them. We spoke of good things to eat and of dancing, but I didn't say anything about liquor since Mr. Warren and the counselors might hear it from The Brig.

The party itself got started after the first carloads of girls had come to the mess hall, and Manuel Rivaz began the record player and then leaped out across the hall, which was cleared of its tables and benches, and chose his friend, May, to dance with, and when they started doing a fast kind of a dance, I had to laugh. I don't know how to dance at all, and don't know the names of dances, but that was a pretty funny dance. Then some other guys went out and chose other girls and pretty soon most of the people there were dancing away, so I went over to the punch, thinking I'd just have a taste, and there was a girl going over so I walked with her and said, "Do you want some punch?" She was quite little, this girl, no more than twelve anyhow, but of course I need them little if I am going to look big, so she was the right size for me. She said, "Okay," so I waited in line and poured two glasses of punch and gave one to her. We walked out to the edge of the hall, which looks down on to the river, and it really did seem like it was going to be a nice party and that we had been missing something. I thought so, that is, until I tasted that punch. If you ever had a yen for pistachio ice cream mixed with gasoline, you just might have liked that punch. I just spat it out and so did this girl, whose name is Irene Mannering. "My God," she said, "what is it?" "Union 76," I said, and we laughed. "How about some Kool-aid?" I suggested, and she liked this idea, so I went over to the line where the smaller kids were.

Then for a while we stood around drinking Kool-aid, and Ham Pumpernil came over and slapped me on the back and said, "A born leader." He was drinking lemon-flavored Kool-aid, to, and I introduced him to Irene. Ham told her, "This is Winston Weyn. He's the youngest guy on the whole S.R.C." She asked me, "Are you a member of the Supreme Revolutionary Committee?" I said, "I'm chairman of the propaganda committee." She said, "You must be at least a captain. Our propaganda chairman is just a lieutenant." "Yes," I said," Lieutenant Wright. She's under me." Then I introduced Ham as Lieutenant Pumpernil, who was communications officer and I called him the "senior member of the propaganda staff," which sounded pretty good, I thought. Irene was very impressed with us. I asked her how things were at Low Pines and if she liked the revolution and she said, "At first most of us didn't like the idea at all, but Susan Langer has told us how it's all in fun and isn't our responsibility anyhow, and I suppose it's true that there's more to do now than there was before." Outside of that, she just shrugged. I got the impression that what she meant was that a lot of the girls felt they were being treated more like grownups, something like that, and could choose what they wanted to do and eat, and say what they felt like saying and so on. But she did seem a little nervous when she asked, "Only, how long is it going to last?" I told her I didn't know, but maybe a few more days, and I said, "Frank, that's General Reilley, he says the revolution isn't even over yet. I guess he means there is some counterrevolutionary activity he's worried about, something like that." I told her I nearly got hooked on the charge of being counterrevolutionary myself, and she opened her eyes to the bursting-point and said, "You *did?*" and I could see that this impressed her even more than me being a member of the S.R.C.

Irene asked me, "Do you know how to dance?" I asked her if she did, and she said, "Come on, I'll teach you a little." She set her glass down on the railing and I was scared, because I'm not the most graceful boy in the world, and anyhow I have never even touched a girl, professionally like that, and so I was nervous. But anyhow, she took me on to the dance floor and tried to show me how to move my feet, but frankly they couldn't make any more sense out of the music than my head could, but I tried to dance for a while and then we went back to finish our Kool-aid.

I spent nearly the whole party with Irene, pointing out my friends and gabbing. Paul Indian danced with about eight girls, but Manuel Rivaz danced with his one girl nearly the whole party—May, that is, who is extremely lovely. I was interested to see that Don Egriss was at the party and he danced a little, too, with a white girl and with a colored girl. Stanley Runk was the first guy to get drunk, I think, but he wasn't the only one. Jerome Blackridge and a few other big guys were pretty noisy, and I believe Eddy Hoag got a little touched by the punch, too. My brother Howard was at the party, and danced quite a bit, and he carried a glass of punch around with him all the time, but I don't think he drank much from it at all because he didn't seem to be drunk.

Around midnight the noise finally started to quiet down and Frank said the party had to end (big moans) and then added, "The next party will be coming up Friday night, same time, same station" (cheers), and then the girls began to leave.

So I walked with Irene out to the station wagon and asked her if she would be my "date" on Friday night, and she said, "Of course," just as though it would never have occurred to her to have to think about it. I felt pretty good.

I guess today wasn't so bad, all in all, because even Don Egriss seemed to enjoy himself at the party, and now that I am on the S.R.C. I guess I'll be able to learn more about what is happening with the revolution.

JUNE 9

The propaganda committee now has to read all the letters the kids write to people outside High Pines, and this is for girls as well as boys, and I have to be sure there is nothing in them that even hints at the revolution. We are encouraging all the kids to try to keep folks from visiting here next Sunday, visitors' day, and so each kid has been required to write at least one letter home. Frank scheduled a big party for Sunday, and has passed around the word that of course we can't have it if visitors come, and so this is keeping kids from suggesting their folks come on up, since even those who aren't interested in the party don't want to get in trouble with the kids who want the party.

But it is a difficult job, reading all those letters, and it is unpleasant to have to censor the letters, because it means going back to the kids and having them write their letters all over again, and some of the kids, especially the smaller ones, write slowly or hate to write or something, and so they fuss.

George Meridel petitioned Frank personally today, asking that everybody be required to say the Pledge of Allegiance and sing the National Anthem every morning, and Frank told him the S.R.C. would consider the petition at its next meeting. George also reminded Frank that I had been reading a book with Marx in it, and it seemed funny to George that the guy who wanted to say the Pledge of Allegiance and sing the National Anthem every morning wasn't even an officer, much less on the S.R.C., while the guy who read Marx was in charge of propaganda, was an officer and a member of the S.R.C. I had to point out that my book was about all kinds of things in politics, and I couldn't understand all of it anyhow, and Frank said it was okay, but maybe I should stick to the Bible, or anyhow not read the parts in my political-philosophers book which are by Marx. So that made me curious about Marx, since he is the only writer in the whole book anyone seems to care about, and this afternoon I began to read the Marx parts, but they are too hard to understand.

Marx writes about the "bourgeoisie" the same way that Thomas Jefferson writes about old George Guelf, King of Britain, and I guess hate has a lot to do with politics. It is very hard to understand what the "bourgeoisie" is, exactly, but it seems to have a lot to do with businessmen, especially businessmen who have their own businesses. I wonder if my father is a member of this "bourgeoisie" and, if so, am I a member of it too? If so, then I guess Marx doesn't like my father or me or my whole family.

Marx also writes some very strange things, just as strange as I have seen in Herodotus. In fact, he seems to be against nearly everything in the world, and he blames everything on the "bourgeoisie." For example, he is against private property, by which I guess he means nobody should even own a house or a piece of land or anything. He is even against having families, though I am not clear on this. He is also against patriotism, I guess, where he writes, "The working men have no country." He is against children inheriting things from their parents. He says Christianity is evil because it makes poverty look like a "blessing" and it teaches people to be satisfied with being poor. He is certainly against a lot. And all I know is, if Marx is against having families and a home, I just don't like him. Maybe I don't get along so well with Howard or even with my father or Mama, but if I have to leave my family in order to understand Marx, well, I don't care to understand him, that's all. It's a shameful idea.

Mostly in this book I have just read Thomas Jefferson, John Stuart Mill and some Henry David Thoreau, although only Thomas Jefferson isn't too difficult for me, and even he is too difficult in some places. Thoreau, I believe, writes the best, but the prettier he writes, the harder he gets, too. And John Stuart Mill reminded me of reading in my book on *Religions of the World* the parts about Confucius. Of course, where I understand Mill, I like him, since he himself seems to like people a great deal and has so much faith in them, but I myself don't know if I could have as much faith as he has in people, since he seems to think nearly everybody is equal enough so that everybody can do fine just by competing with others. But that would only mean that people who are born either strong or smart could get the nicest things, and ordinary people who are not so strong or so smart could not get the nicest things, just because nature had not blessed them so much. It's hard to figure out, but somehow this doesn't seem like "equal rights" to me. I wonder if this has anything to do with why Marx is against businessmen, since businessmen are always competing in this way. Well, I just can't know everything and, frankly, it makes me mad. I am going to stop writing now, and read.

JUNE 10

Today I'm kind of scared again. I had to attend a special meeting of the S.R.C., attended only by Frank, Stanley, Susan, Blackridge and me. The subject was the continuation of the revolution, and the need for loyalty. I was given a special assignment, which was to drive into Wellberg with Jerome Blackridge. I had to get a map of Wellberg and locate certain buildings on it, such as the city hall and courthouse and schools and police stations. I asked Frank why I had to do this and he seemed nervous and blinked his purple eyes a lot and scowled and said, "It's a special course in geography, Win. Don't ask questions. What the hell have questions got to do with loyalty? We need the map and that's enough for you to know. The thing will go like this. Jerry goes into town after some groceries—anything— it doesn't matter, and you go along for the ride. If anyone gets interested in you guys, Jerry is a counselor up here and you, Win, because you're small, no one's going to suspect you of being too curious about anything. Anyhow, Win, you're chairman of the propaganda committee, and this assignment has plenty to do with propaganda."

I shook my head to say, "I don't understand why we need such a map, though."

"Do you have to know everything, Sonny?" asked Stanley Runk. "You're going to wear your brain out by

114

the time you're fifteen. It'll be ridiculous. Girls will shun you. This assignment is the Fountain of Youth, small crap. Jump in and shut up."

I can't talk to Stanley at all, but I asked Frank, "We aren't going to invade Wellberg or anything like that, are we?"

Frank just wouldn't discuss it, he blinked some more and said, "Are you questioning me again, Win?"

He was on the edge of losing his temper so I was afraid to say anything except, "No."

Stanley Runk lost his own temper at that, saying, "You say, *no sir,* kid!"

"Shut up, Runk!" snapped Frank.

"What do you mean, shut up?" Stanley turned on Frank. "You ain't got an ounce more rank than I have and you been trying to pull rank over me lately. You looking for trouble, Reilley?"

Frank glared at Stanley, and I'm surprised Stanley didn't just burn up from the way Frank glared at him.

"Listen, Reilley," Stanley shook his finger at Frank, "don't forget whose revolution this is. It ain't your revolution, it's *my* revolution, it was my idea and you couldn't have done it without me. And when I decide it's over, Reilley, it's over. Done. Right then. So don't press me."

Frank glared at Stanley a minute more, then took out a cigarette and lit it and at last he seemed to get control of his nerves or something, and he said, "All right, Win. Be ready to go with Jerry within an hour."

I said, "Okay," but I was really worried.

"Yeah," muttered Stanley, "and Blackridge, you pick up some gin while you're in Wellberg. We got a party tonight. Give him some extra dough, Reilley."

Frank inhaled at his cigarette and didn't look at

Stanley and said very softly, "We have enough gin for three parties and we're running low on cash."

Stanley, who had sat down in a chair, stood up again. "I said to get some more gin, Reilley."

Frank looked at Stanley at last. "You got money of your own, Runk?"

Stanley shook his head slowly and I was scared he was going to pull out his knife but he just said, "You be careful, Reilley. You be careful. We ain't brothers." Then Stanley just stared at Frank for a time and Frank stared back, but not with that hot glare of his, he was now cold and hateful-looking and I couldn't help shuddering. Then Stanley turned and left the room.

For a time no one spoke and then Frank really shocked me by saying to Blackridge, "I want you to arrest Runk, Jerry."

Blackridge blinked.

"I want you to arrest him, Jerry," said Frank. "Find a good time and a good place and get him to The Brig before you leave for Wellberg. Be careful and bring me his knife. Gag him if he wants to complain too much. You understand?"

Blackridge nodded, but looked a little numb.

"Okay," said Frank. "That's all."

So I pushed off to my cabin, not wanting to be anywhere around when Jerome Blackridge arrested Stanley Runk. I would have thought it might take ten guys to arrest Stanley, but Jerome Blackridge told me, when we drove into Wellberg, that it had been easy and that Stanley wept when his knife was taken away, he actually wept tears, and Blackridge laughed and laughed about it. He said the counselors and cooks were real surprised to see who they were getting for company. I asked how Mr. Warren and everyone was, and Blackridge stopped laughing and glanced at me a little curiously, like it was none of my business at all, but then he said I shouldn't worry about the prisoners, they liked The Brig fine. He said the R.P. (the Revolutionary Police) were under strict orders to treat all prisoners well, and take care of them from food to laundry. But Blackridge said he was sorry to have had to leave camp just then, when Stanley the Punk would be trying to accommodate himself to such companions as Mr. Taber and Mr. Laudenseller.

I studied the map of Wellberg most of the ride in, a map we got at a gas station, and I saw it was a pretty small town. Already marked on the map were a few places, such as the city hall and courthouse, but I had to walk around awhile to locate the police stations (two of them, one at the courthouse and one way out on Crab Creek Road), and the telephone building, which was right across from the courthouse and so not too hard to find. I also noted the place where I saw a policeman driving a patrol car, and the hour, and where I saw a policeman walking, because these seemed the kind of "official" things Frank was interested in knowing. Then I also marked down where some stores were, and a bank, and a big official-looking house of some kind, and all the schools. At last, we drove back to High Pines and I gave the map to Frank.

Frank studied the map for just a couple minutes and then he gave me a very warm kind of look, like we were very close or something, and he said, "Major Weyn, that's a damned good job."

"Am I a major?" I asked.

Frank said, "Hell, we lost a general this morning. I guess we can afford to pay a major."

Blackridge frowned but I felt good and I said, laughing, "What is my new salary?"

Frank said, "You keep it inside that active little

117

brain of yours, Win, but you may actually have a salary before we finish this revolution. I'm working on it."

That flabbergasted me, that really did.

"Just keep it to yourself," Frank said, sounding nearly angry, as if he was sorry he had mentioned it at all. "But I mean to see that the guys who are most valuable around here don't have to do all they're doing for nothing. Just keep doing as good as you're doing."

Well, I don't know where Frank intends to get any money to pay anybody, unless he himself has more money than I think, and I was wondering how much money he meant to give me. Of course, I couldn't help feeling good about being a major. This means there are only three people in the whole revolution with higher rank than mine, and these are Frank and Blackridge and Susan Langer, and now I am the same rank as Manuel Rivaz and Edna Kay.

"You know why I raised your rank?" Frank asked me before I left the Administration Building. I told him I didn't and he went on, "Because you always do things *better* than you're told. You do *more* than just obey orders. You're smart, Win. You think." All the while, Blackridge kind of leered at me and I could see he was thinking, too. So I saluted and left the Presence.

Ham, finding out I was a major, asked me, after reminding me I am a "born leader," if I couldn't get him promoted to captain, since he was really serving as Communications Officer for both camps instead of just one. Being captain would get him on the S.R.C., so I told him I would ask Frank about it.

There is a dreadful rumor that was going around today that the reason Stanley Runk got arrested is that he actually stabbed a counselor, but of course that doesn't make sense, because I was there when Frank asked Blackridge to arrest Stanley. But it sounded like a dangerous rumor, so I reported it to Frank tonight and he said, "Let's just say I put Runk in The Brig because I'm afraid he's lunatic enough to try such a thing"—but I could see Frank was disturbed by the rumor. He paced a lot and was even sweating, and sometimes when he was looking at me I was sure he wasn't seeing me at all, and for a while I thought he was feeling sick. For a time Frank began to talk to me about things he hadn't spoken before, I guess it was because we were alone. He talked about Plato and asked me about my Herodotus and then he talked awhile about his father, who had been a minister, and I don't think he liked his father much, from the way he talked. He asked me if I was religious, but didn't give me a chance to answer, he began to talk about places in the Bible that he doubted were reasonable. Then, all at once, he just put his hand to the back of his neck and stopped talking and stared at me for a while. It was some minutes, I guess, before he had another word to say, and then he asked me, "You know what I want, Win?" and answered himself, "I want to make everything better. Right. Perfect. Can you understand that?" But even then he didn't let me answer, he just chuckled from down deep in his lungs somewhere and looked at me as if he couldn't have expected a kid my age to know what he had in mind. And I guess that was about the size of it, although I would have liked to ask him what he meant. Only he didn't want to talk any more, he just said, "We better get over to the party, Major."

The party tonight was pretty much the same as the party on Wednesday night, except that we had a lot of doughnuts this time instead of cookies. I didn't spend all of my time at the party, actually, because I went for a walk with Irene, but I can say that the party was pretty noisy, because no matter where we went, we heard it. Irene is really quite pretty, I think. She lives near where Paul Indian lives, and knows him a little. I suppose, in a way, she's my girl friend now.

JUNE 11

Well, we've just got so many troubles now I can't think how we'll ever get over them. I don't even know where to begin today.

In the first place, Jerome Blackridge has had to arrest John Mason, who is a member of his own Revolutionary Police, because a girl has accused John Mason of doing something bad to her. I don't know the girl, but Susan Langer came over here to make the charge and we had a special meeting of the S.R.C. about it.

Susan demanded that John Mason be arrested and kept in The Brig until the end of the revolution, when he should be given over to the police. And I, myself, said it was probably time to just call off the revolution. Both Frank and Jerome Blackridge said we were wrong, and they told us a number of girls had "gone into the woods" with guys from High Pines, and that it was hard to know just where to draw the line, but Frank said it was especially important to keep the revolution free of the "taint" of that kind of thing. He said he didn't want any trouble with the police, and if John Mason had to be punished, then the S.R.C. itself would have to decide his punishment. Susan said that the revolution won't last long enough to punish John Mason the way he deserves, unless he was executed. So Frank, who was wearing a very pained expression all through the meeting, groaned a little and went back to trying to make a case for John Mason because so many girls, as he said, had been willing to go off "into the woods" and he said the thing to do isn't to punish at all, but to make new laws which will keep this sort of thing from happening again.

"What good will laws be without punishment?" asked Susan madly.

Jerome Blackridge said he agreed with this attitude (and I was wondering if he was anxious to beat John Mason with his belt, or maybe be the one to execute him, even though Mason is his friend). Then Paul Indian suggested that maybe I was right and it was time to end the revolution because, as he said, "No one was supposed to get hurt."

Frank took to looking at me, as if I had spoken instead of Paul, and his eyes still looked sad, like someone had been insulting him, and then he said, "We have to handle this for ourselves."

"Well," I finally suggested, "why not ask the girl what ought to be done with John Mason?"

"Sure," said Paul, "and what if she says to kill him?"

Frank shook his head and all at once didn't look sad any more, but just nervous and angry. "It's not a bad idea," he said, and even though Susan Langer was moody about the idea, she agreed to arrange a meeting of the S.R.C. at Low Pines, at which both the girl and John Mason will be present, and that will be sort of a trial for John Mason. The meeting will be around ten o'clock tomorrow morning.

I don't blame Frank for being so edgy, and I should think he must be nearly ready to call off the revolution himself, even if everything *is* in such a mess. He is very worried about something else, too, and told us that word of the revolution may have leaked out. He says it is just a possibility, but that he has received news of some "odd" activities in Wellberg and it may have something to do with us. He said he wouldn't explain any of this right away, but if word has been leaked out and he finds out who did it, he'll get worse than John Mason gets.

I asked Frank what kind of activities there were in Wellberg, but he just said that it was an attitude down there, and it meant something was up, and it might mean trouble for us and it might not, but the point was, he said, we have to be prepared for any kind of operation against us. He made it very clear to us that he didn't want the revolution to end with any loose strings. It had to end as playfully as it began or else too many kids would be in serious trouble. By that, he meant it certainly couldn't end right now. He told us we had to clear up the problems of having held adults in The Brig for nearly a week, which would be done by negotiating with the prisoners so that they wouldn't care to call it anything like "kidnapping"; and there was the problem with John Mason; and the problem of fraternization between High Pines and Low Pines which had to be investigated and controlled so that no more trouble would come out of it; and he really did imply that we have broken some real laws and might even go to jail for it.

I had to say, "I haven't broken any laws," feeling sure I have not, at least no laws I know about.

Paul seemed really broken up by what Frank was saying because, after all, his father is a policeman. "I sure as hell didn't break any laws," Paul insisted to Frank.

But Frank said, "I'm sorry, you guys," and he studied all of our faces for some moments. "I really am

123

sorry, because I like all of you and have depended on all of you and know that all the kids in this revolution can go right on depending on you. That's the kind of kids you are. Loyal. But it's pointless to be loyal and dumb, like a dog. We'd better be loyal and smart, and recognize facts. We're the leaders of this revolution. We're responsible. I'm more responsible than anyone else, that's certain, and I'm in more trouble than anyone else. That's good, that's the way I want it, and I'll keep carrying all the responsibility I can, and I won't be afraid to do that because I'll know, at least in my own heart, that I'm going to be trying to do the right thing all the way by everyone involved in what we've done. But it won't pay you to think the responsibility ends with me. After all, I couldn't have made this revolution all by myself, nor am I the only guy here to reap the rewards of fun and rank out of it. I'm going to do all I can to protect you, but you'll help to protect yourselves by facing up to facts. We have troubles. They have to be cleared up, or you'll be charged with some portion of their responsibility."

This kept all of us quiet for some time. At last I said, "What could they do to me?" I was really feeling dizzy.

"Oh," said Frank, "don't open up your sweat glands, Win. No one's going to execute you. Maybe they'd stick you in a school for a little while, that's the worst they could do. A year, maybe."

I just wanted to cry.

And Paul Indian had tears in his eyes, I saw them, and he said, "My father will lose his job."

"Aw, who's going to miss a cop?" asked Jerome Blackridge, who has a heart as big as Africa and just about that weedy.

Frank stood up behind his desk and slapped the top

of the desk with his hand. "Shut up!" He glared at us briefly, then sat down again and covered his eyes with his hand, and when he took his hand away his face looked only a little sad again. "Nobody's going to jail, nobody's going to lose a job. I wasn't trying to scare you, I didn't really think you guys would scare so easy. I was only describing some of our current problems. They're problems of the revolution, and so long as the revolution has problems, the revolution isn't over. And we haven't lost it, and I'm not intending to lose it."

"What do you expect us to do?" demanded Paul. "Fight the United States Army?"

"No, I don't expect you to fight the United States Army," Frank snapped right back at him. "What I expect you to do is keep your head the same way I'm keeping mine. I expect you to be prepared."

"Just like the boy scouts," said Jerome Blackridge.

"The thing is," Frank went on, "this place has got to be made invulnerable, absolutely invulnerable, to any kind of infiltration. We've got to make a kind of fort out of these camps. We've got to create an attitude of readiness and willingness in these camps, we've got to create an *esprit de corps.*"

"What's that?" asked Blackridge. "An army?"

"No, it's loyalty," said Frank. "That's what we need, something to draw all of us together so that no one betrays the rest of us. We've got to be in a position at least strong enough so that they have to let us surrender, and not in any position so weak that they can come in and take us straight off to Alcatraz. In short, a position from which we can make certain demands, create terms. Don't get bleary-eyed, any of you, I know what I'm talking about. After all, we have certain advantages on our side and we mean to make use of them. For example, we have a tremendous advantage in that we're so young—most of us just kids. Nobody's going to send planes over and bomb us or strafe us, nobody's going to start shooting guns in here."

"Oh my God," moaned Paul.

Frank just stared at Paul, then looked down at the desk and mumbled, "For all I know, there hasn't even been a leak. I only say, let's fix things up so we're in as little trouble as possible. Just let's be prepared. If anyone here thinks he can do a better job than me or be more dedicated than me, prove it and I'll give you the whole revolution. Until then," he looked up again, "do as I say."

There was a big, long silence—a sort of sticky silence.

Then Susan Langer said in a small voice, "Maybe we should just surrender. God, Frank, from the girls' point of view, we just aren't worried about what happens to John Mason."

"Yeah?" growled Blackridge. "Well, that's tough, Susie. You remember who's running this revolution and remember another thing: you're in trouble, yourself. You're the leader of the girls' camp and you're more responsible than any other dame in the revolution."

"Susie," Frank said very softly, waving Blackridge's words aside, "it isn't what happens to John Mason that concerns me. It's what happens to *most* people here. We have to get things to the point where the fewest possible of us have any dancing to do to judicial tunes. You get me?" She shook her head. "Never mind then," Frank looked at his desk again. "Look, don't worry, any of you. Probably there's no leak. Probably we have time to make our terms right here, with the counselors. Probably we have plenty of time to set things right. After all, the guys who run this camp aren't going to be anxious to publicize how easy it is for things to blow up in their faces, how easy it is for their kids to get into bad trouble, for their boys to get to their girls. They'll make terms. So maybe there was no leak and maybe we got all the time in the world to end the revolution peacefully, to set things straight, to just go home." He looked up, scowling. "Fine! Great! I'm only saying that maybe there was a leak and, if there was, I want us to be prepared, so that we have the least possible degree of trouble after the revolution is over. So try to keep your brains in your heads and your heads pinned to your shoulders for a while, will you? At least long enough for me to point out some of the problems we have!"

"Good God," Paul moaned again, "are there more problems?"

Frank got up and began to pace as he spoke. "We have internal problems, don't we? I mean, we're the only people in the whole revolution aware of its real problems, just us, in this room. This means we've got plenty of educating to do. Win, we're depending a lot on you. We have to make every kid at both camps not just a member of the militia, but an *alert* member of the militia. And, so far as we can, a *trained* member of the militia. And, just as important, a *dedicated* member of the militia. And then we have supply problems to work out. I still don't know all the ways of getting supplies for both camps, but we're running low in some quarters, and we aren't wealthy, either; well, this is my problem and I'll work it out. But we have about thirty-five dollars left between both camps, and thirty-five dollars isn't much money if we run into serious shortages in supplies. And, as a matter of fact, it's going to take money to run this revolution day by day from now on. I've mentioned it before, and I'll mention it again: I want things to be *good* in this revolution, not bad. I want the kids to be dedicated for a reason, not just because we say so. I want to provide incentive, and money is the only thing that buys incentive. Well, let this problem hold for a couple of days. But it won't hold longer than that, and then this is going to be a problem to fall on your shoulders, too, Win."

"Shoulders," chuckled Blackridge.

"We've got to do two things about money." Frank looked at me directly, only kind of abstractly, his fingers playing with his adam's apple. "First, everybody at High Pines has to contribute to the revolution, and at Low Pines, too. Now, by that I mean, no matter who has how much, *all* money is turned over to the revolution. This isn't to be confiscation, and it isn't taxes or anything, it's a loan."

"Like war bonds?" I asked.

Frank grinned. "Exactly. Now, that's great. Sure, call them Revolution Bonds. Win, make up some cards of some kind on your mimeo, leaving a space for how much money each kid gives, and let's say the card will be worth that much money plus ten per cent at the end of the revolution."

"But how will we pay them back?" asked Susan Langer.

"We'll pay them back," Frank frowned. "And remember that the money got in this way is to be spent for the benefit of everybody. We aren't collecting for ourselves or anything like that. Anyhow, we aren't going to get much this way. What will we get in High Pines, for instance, if each kid had fifty cents? Not even fifty bucks. This brings me to something more important, Win. I want you to get the kids to write home for money. What we're doing up here is trying to make things as right as possible for kids, so let their parents support this revolution. Try to get the kids to beg their parents to buy them another month up here, only be sure they ask their parents to pay in cash. You can think up something to make it sound all right. Have them say that a month costs twenty-five bucks by check, but just twenty by cash because of bookkeeping problems, something like that, any God-damned thing. Just make sure they get some weepy letters off, sounding like they really *want* to spend another month here. This is important," and Frank had come right up to me and was looking right down in my eyes, very excited, "because without money, we're finished. We got trouble. Win, you understand what I want?" He suddenly took my shoulder and squeezed it. "You understand how important your job is? It will work." He gazed at me some seconds and then let go of my shoulder and I began to rub it, since it was hurting a bit. Frank nodded, seeming to think he had made his point so long as I had to rub my shoulder. "Later on we can make use of some of the camp money in Wellberg. It will take a little longer, I guess, to get Mrs. Knute to co-operate in this."

"You should leave her to me," said Jerome Blackridge. "I wouldn't have to touch her. I'd just scare her." Blackridge was beginning to remind me more and more of Stanley Runk all the time.

"What money is that?" asked Paul.

"The Pines Camps money. Most of it isn't up here, unfortunately, but," said Frank, "there's an account in Wellberg which has nearly two thousand bucks. I figure that money came from the parents of kids up here, and it rightfully belongs to the kids, and just now the revolution is acting as the kids' guardians, so we should have access to it when the kids need something. Mrs. Knute doesn't see it that way."

"Can't Mr. Warren touch it?" asked Susan Langer.

Frank just looked at the floor, then went and sat behind his desk again, and shrugged. "Sure, I guess so. Well, we'll get their cooperation eventually and that will be nearly two thousand dollars to help us along."

Paul shook his head. "You're talking about robbery."

Frank shot Paul a very nasty glance.

"Robbery, hell," said Jerome Blackridge. "That money belongs to all of us. Why should we starve because an old lady like that thinks she's still running things up here?"

"Shut up, Jerry," said Frank.

"I still say it's wrong," said Paul, and I was agreeing with him.

"Okay! Frank hissed at us. "It's robbery! But I'm in charge. Does anyone doubt that?"

Well, no one was willing to make any claims against Frank, so he blinked at us after a bit, put some notes on his desk and examined them. I had been making notes, too, and so I studied my own, and muttered, "I sure am going to be busy."

Frank didn't look up. "We'll all be busy." He went on looking at his papers. Finally he faced us again and said, "There's been too much moodiness around. I think a little reorganization will help that. We have to broaden the system of rank. We don't need cabins, maybe, but we do need platoons, and I want a boys' brigade and a girls' brigade formed. We need insignia. We'll appoint lieutenants and we'll also select the right guys for corporals and sergeants. Susan, I want you to get some girls together who know something about design and sewing and present me with some suggestions for insignia for all ranks. Indian, start getting the word around we're reorganizing and that we mean to make some of the best people around here lieutenants, and that soon everyone is going to be taking an active and interesting part in the revolution. Let them know there will be little rewards all along the way for good service. Susan, you and Jerry get me a list of recommendations for new officer appointments. And whatever your job is, whatever you do, you make it sound like fun, God damn it!" Frank went back to his notes, biting at his fingers a little, and then he just sort of muttered, "That's all."

After the S.R.C. meeting, I called a meeting of my own committee and explained that the revolution was going on and that it faced some strange problems which I couldn't describe completely, but that everything was all right. I told them we would need money for supplies for a few days and it was our job to collect it, and I explained about Revolution Bonds and got a lot of moans for my trouble. Bob McCarthy said, "Who's supposed to pay it back?" I told him, "That's already taken care of, according to Frank," and so there was nothing to do but order them to help me. So we made up notices and went from cabin to cabin posting them, the notices giving information about Revolution Bonds and telling how any withholding of money at this time could betray the revolution and might be counterrevolutionary. Then we hiked over to the girls' camp and posted notices there, and I saw Irene for a while.

We planned to collect the money tomorrow, to give everyone time to make all the objections they had to make among themselves, I hope.

Next, I began preparing letters to post in each cabin tomorrow, to be used as models for everyone to write home and ask for money, requesting their folks to let the kids stay another month at High Pines or Low Pines.

All this work took me and my committee nearly the

whole day, and even then my work wasn't done, because after dinner I had to prepare some lists of all the officers of the revolution and make a mimeograph of another notice which is being posted all around the camps, and which has been read a couple of times over the loudspeakers. (At both camps, too, because Ham has now set up loudspeakers at both camps, and tomorrow is actually going to try to string cord all the way from the girls' camp to the boys' camp, so that both camps can be talked to at the same time by one person.) This is the proclamation, I guess you'd call it, that Frank made up today:

ATTENTION!

General Frank Reilley, Commander of Revolutionary Forces, Chairman of the Supreme Revolutionary Committee, has announced that, with the continuing co-operation of the Revolutionary Militia, the Revolution is solving its problems and progressing satisfactorily. The continued co-operation of the Militia is commanded in the formation of two Revolutionary Brigades, the High Pines Brigade and the Low Pines Brigade. Special training of the Militia will begin on Monday morning, with special awards offered for outstanding effort and ability in support of the Revolution.

Officers of the Revolution

General Frank Reilley, Commander, All Forces
Colonel Susan Langer, Commander, Low Pines Brigade
Colonel Jerome Blackridge, Chief, Revolutionary Police
Major Manuel Rivaz, Adjutant, General Reilley

Major Edna Kay, Revolutionary Police, Low Pines
Major Winston Weyn, Chairman, Propaganda
Captain Dick Richardson, Sub-Chief, Revolutionary
    Police
Captain Jean Laughlin, Adjutant, Colonel Langer
Captain Paul Indian, Liaison, High Pines
Captain Bernice Royer, Liaison, Low Pines
Lieutenant George Meridel, Brigade Adjutant, High
    Pines
Lieutenant Marian Jay, Brigade Adjutant, Low Pines
Lieutenant Evelyn Wright, Propaganda, Low Pines
Lieutenant Ham Pumpernil, Communications
Lieutenant Alice Epson, Supply and Kitchen Officer
Lieutenant Bob Daly, First High Pines Platoon
Lieutenant Fred Elston, Second High Pines Platoon
Lieutenant Howard Weyn, Third High Pines Platoon
Lieutenant Eddy Hoag, Fourth High Pines Platoon
Lieutenant Oly Anderson, Fifth High Pines Platoon
Lieutenant Erika Zigeuns, First Low Pines Platoon
Lieutenant Irene Mannering, Second Low Pines Pla-
    toon
Lieutenant Arlene Platt, Third Low Pines Platoon
Lieutenant Roberta Funston, Fourth Low Pines Pla-
    toon

Work for an N.C.O. Appointment!

You can just guess how much I approved of some of
those appointments. (Of course, I shouldn't complain
too much, because I recommended Irene, myself. Also,
I tried to get Frank to make Ham a captain, but he
only said he would think about it, and that the S.R.C.
was getting pretty big now that Dick Richardson was
on it, too.)

There's one thing I didn't mention, which occurs to

me now, and that is that Frank really gained a certain amount of support and respect after arresting Stanley Runk, because a lot of guys distrusted Stanley. And Frank's decision to arrest John Mason was popular for the same reason, of course. One thing I have to say for Frank, that I couldn't ever have said for Stanley, is that he does seem to have a head on his shoulders, and knows what to say and when to say it, and it is hard to get around him. What I can't figure out about his head, though, is where it is going. He organizes everything and seems to reward service, so that I'm a major even though I'm a little guy, but it's still hard to see where Frank and his head and the whole revolution is really going.

JUNE 12

Early this morning we went around and collected money from both camps, cabin by cabin. (Howard said, "You can contribute for our family, Major.") I collected nearly eighty dollars in a big flour sack, mostly in small change, nickels and dimes and plenty of pennies, and I turned it over to Frank. I gave out more than a hundred and fifty Revolution Bonds in all.

I noticed that a lot of kids really do seem more interested in the revolution now that the ranks are being passed out, and a lot of them want to be noncommissioned officers, and they keep asking what kind of awards will be given for doing good work, but I wasn't able to tell them, not knowing myself.

The meeting of Revolutionary Officers was at eleven o'clock this morning. The only thing we discussed, though, was getting in the recommendations for noncommissioned officers, and the training which is to begin tomorrow. The training will only consist of drilling up in the meadow, to begin with, and calisthenics, and talks by some of the officers, including me, which are called *Orientation*. This was the first meeting I attended in a long time which also included Howard— to say nothing of the new Lieutenant, George Meridel.

The party began today with a short talk by Frank, to celebrate the one-week anniversary of the revolution. He really spoke very enthusiastically, and yet at the same time very gently, and he said how important it is to continue the work of the revolution at this time, and about how much he admired everyone for doing all they were doing, and how he meant to see that everyone had all he needed and wanted so long as the revolution lasted. He spoke of fun and more fun, and loyalty and more loyalty, and courage and more courage. He made a good speech, I guess; it sounded intelligent, anyhow, even though—when I thought about it—I couldn't say that he had said anything very definite about anything at all.

Manuel Rivaz was about to turn on the record player but had to stop because Jerome Blackridge got up on the platform and shouted, "Come on, you schmucks, three cheers for Frank Reilley, who took this kiddy-camp and made it a circus," and so there were three cheers for Frank, who looked very surprised and even a little hurt to see what was happening; I thought he looked more like a clergyman than General Reilley, but at last the music got started and everyone began to dance and the party went on and on.

I took another walk with Irene, and also with Manuel Rivaz and his girl, May Chasims, and with Ham and Paul and a girl Paul knows named Helen. We all walked quite far into the woods, farther than we ever went before. I don't even suppose any human ever walked some of the places we walked, because we had to push through so much shrubbery and bushes and stuff, and there were no paths part of the way. We found a little pond out there, and some caves—I guess these must be the caves Mr. Warren talked about—but we decided not to stay there because the place just didn't smell good and Paul said it smelled like the elephants came there to die, but Rivaz said it smelled more like they came there to crap, which I think embarrassed Irene.

Well, we all went around the pond and away from the caves and sat down for a time, talking about the revolution and things, and most of us agreed it was getting pretty long and probably we ought to end it in a couple days, no matter how much trouble we were in, just because we might get into still more trouble if we kept it going. On the other hand, we all agreed we weren't anxious to go to jail, either, so it seemed like a really difficult problem.

We talked about what ought to be done to John Mason, but Manuel Rivaz said it didn't matter about what we thought should be done with Mason or whether Frank Reilley agreed with Susan or not, because Mason was sure to wind up with the police for what he did, and no terms the revolution could hope to make would change that, simply because no one was going to change the United States laws for us. They would even bomb us before doing that, Manuel said. So we all agreed we were in a pretty bad mess and that it was probably more Frank Reilley's fault than anyone else's, just because he was such a good organizer and such a good talker and has kept the revolution going practically by himself. I never thought of this until Manuel said so, but it is true, because I can't think who else in this camp would go and sit behind Mr. Warren's desk and make all those decisions and demands. And then, people *obey* Frank for some reason, but when you stop to think about it, *why* do they obey him? After all, Frank couldn't do anything about it if no one obeyed him, not even with Jerome Blackridge's help. It's kind of weird. Ham should be calling Frank the "born leader," not me.

Of course, even though it's maybe Frank's fault more

than anyone else's, we had to agree we'd be in still more of a mess if Frank wasn't around. The revolution was Stanley Runk's idea, to begin with, or that's what Stanley said (and Frank never denied it), and if Stanley was still General—say it was him who arrested Frank, instead of the reverse—then I don't think things would be in any order at all.

I was surprised to hear Manuel Rivaz saying these things, though. I thought he was very close to Frank and all for continuing the revolution, but to me he sounded pretty morose on the subject.

Tonight I was hanging around with Don Egriss awhile, and he's more disgusted with the revolution than anyone, because he told me that he is going to leave the camp. He said, "You wouldn't report me, would you, kid?" I told him I wouldn't, but I would be scared to leave the camp so long as Jerome Blackridge was head of the R.P., and after all, I said, Don knew they weren't awfully fond of him. Don said he didn't care, and couldn't see any point in sticking around longer because there was nothing in it for him. I asked if he was going to squeal on Frank and the revolution. He said he didn't know yet, but he'd think about it after he left. I told him a lot of guys would just as soon call the revolution off now, but it seemed like it was too late and that every single one of us was in some kind of trouble. Don just shrugged. I said, "When are you going?" He shook his head. "I don't guess the chairman of the propaganda committee around here would be the first guy I'd give the details to." That hurt me, I hadn't expected him to say such a thing, and I guess I looked hurt, because he said, more softly, "I don't know when I'm heading out, kid. Why? You want to try it with me?" I thought about that and said, "I guess I better not. I sure don't want to be a martyr or anything." Don nodded and grinned, it was the first time I saw him grin in a long time, and he said, "That's the right idea, kid. That's what I don't want to be, either."

I read today from both Herodotus and my political-philosophers book, but not from the Bible. In fact, I have only read from my Bible a couple times since coming to High Pines. I was reading more from John Stuart Mill, who is a strong "individualist" and I have been trying to figure out how he would feel about our revolution. He says that the "individual is sovereign" over himself, so that I can see he calls us wrong to lock anyone up (but what about real criminals who get put in prisons?). Of course, he also says there are people too young and too old to take care of themselves, and they should be "protected against their own actions." It is hard to apply that to the revolution, because both before and since the revolution we have not been "protected against our own actions" and, in a sense, we have been more "sovereign" over ourselves since the revolution, because the kids get to do a lot more things that they themselves really want to do, the things they call fun. And just to have had a revolution, we weren't being "protected against our own actions." I wonder how people can be "protected" against their actions anyhow, seeing as how it takes only a couple guys and maybe one knife to make a whole revolution.

Question: could we have had the revolution without the knife? Was this whole revolution made by one knife? What a scary thought, because everybody can buy knives.

Speaking of knives, Frank Reilley has Stanley's knife in his drawer, and I mention this because I saw it there, and saw something else too: a gun. Frank told me to keep quiet about it, and said it is a .38 revolver which belongs to Mr. Warren. He said it is better no one knows there is a gun around, which I think is right.

Now I have to write something I don't like to write, but it happened. The S.R.C. took a vote after the officers' meeting and they decided to accept George Meridel's petition for everyone to say the Pledge of Allegiance and sing the National Anthem every morning. Every morning! Well, George Meridel did so much squawking about it at the officers' meeting that they took the vote right after, and believe it or not, Meridel is now thinking of asking them to do it every evening just after dinner, also. So now everyone is supposed to be up and dressed and down at the flagpole in the Quad by eight o'clock. And I was the *only one* to vote against this in the end. Even Paul Indian voted for it (because, as he said, everyone else was voting for it anyhow, so it wouldn't do any good to vote against it, and he said maybe it wasn't such a bad idea anyhow so long as there was a real flag). But I'm against it, because I've been thinking about this quite a bit, and since I'm an atheist I'm going right on fighting George Meridel and the whole S.R.C. I suppose it makes me selfish, but after all the Pledge of Allegiance makes people stand up and say they recognize a God, whereas I don't recognize a God at all. And so this means that the Pledge of Allegiance really doesn't give "liberty for all" as it talks about, since it doesn't give me the liberty to *not* believe in God. I have noticed that John Stuart Mill and others seem to think it is an individual's own right not to believe in God, and I just suppose it is wrong to make an individual stand up and say he believes in something he doesn't believe in. Anyhow, religion isn't supposed to be the business of government, according to Thomas Jefferson and everybody, or even the business of teachers or companies or anyone. So it seems to me I am right to be against any rule which is going to make me stand up and tell a lie, right in public. Because that isn't freedom of speech, or freedom of religion, or freedom of anything, if I am forced to lie.

But the thing is, can I convince the S.R.C. of all of this, because if I can, then maybe they will decide to go against George Meridel's petition after all, on the basis that the Pledge of Allegiance is un-American, because it violates my freedom of religion! Of course, I will then have the same trouble with the last verse of the National Anthem, where it says, "In God is our trust," and even on pennies and nickels and coins it says that, so I guess I won't be able to win my fight. God seems to be on everything that has anything to do with the United States Government, and for a country with religious freedom, people sure haven't got much choice about whether they want God written all over everything or not. Having thought of all these things today, it has made me very sad. I can't explain it. I feel disappointed. I mean, how can I fight the S.R.C. when the whole government of the United States seems to be supporting it?

I guess there really isn't religious freedom in America, after all. I will have to talk to my Uncle Giles about these things, because I'm all mixed up about it. Unless they put me in reform school and don't let me talk to anyone, that is. That's scary. I will lose my citizenship if I go to jail. Maybe I have no freedom any more, anyhow. If they put me in reform school, the only thing I can do, I guess, is write letters trying to explain these things to the President and to Senators and the people who run the Un-American Activities Committee in Washington D.C., and maybe they will help me.

And I am never going to say the Pledge of Allegiance again! I don't care if they hang me for it.

JUNE 13

Trouble, trouble, trouble. Every day it seems the troubles get worse and there seem to be more of them. It was just a bad day.

First of all, I lost a public argument with George Meridel over his Pledge of Allegiance—and why? Here is why: because he pointed out that the writings by Jefferson I quoted were in the very same book as some writings by Karl Marx. I asked him what that had to do with it, and he said that, even if he understood what I was talking about he wouldn't trust it, because maybe it is a Communist book, and he even said: "Maybe you're a Communist."

I said it was an American book and showed it to him, and I asked: "Are you calling Thomas Jefferson a Communist?"

He said, "Are you going to prove that Jefferson really wrote that?"

How could I prove that? I couldn't even prove that Marx wrote the parts by Marx, or Thoreau wrote the parts by Thoreau. But what makes me feel just stupid is, even if I hadn't lost that argument with Meridel, I still wouldn't have been able to do anything about his rule, because nobody really understood what I was talking about anyhow. They are Americans and they don't even understand Thomas Jefferson, who wrote the Constitution!

Frank *said* he understood, but I don't believe he did. What Frank said was, "I understand, Win, and maybe you have a point, but we didn't write the Pledge of Allegiance, we just say it, so why not just say it like the rest of us?"

I said, "I'll never say it again, not even if they hang me for it."

Meridel then tried to make a case out of that, saying he wondered just why I would *not* want to say the Pledge of Allegiance or sing the last verse of the National Anthem, just like he hadn't understood one word I said, which I am sure he didn't, so I said: "I didn't say I didn't *want* to, I said I *wouldn't,* because it just happens to violate my freedom, and so I also refuse to sing the last verse of the National Anthem."

Everyone was quiet and I could see no one really liked what I was saying. I guess they were afraid God and George Washington were both about to gang up on them or something, and Paul finally muttered, "Win, you really talk too much."

Frank, who was grinning a little, but a cold and untelling grin, said, "Hell, I don't know anything about religion, when I stop to think about it. Maybe there's a God, maybe there isn't. If there is, he never pulled *me* out of any jams before. But I can't see the S.R.C. is the place to decide whether or not there's a God, and if there is one, you can see he must be pretty mad at me for directing a revolution right in the middle of the Sunday services. But what the hell, if people want to believe in God, that's their business, Win."

"I didn't say people shouldn't believe in God," I told Frank, and now I was angry, myself. "I just said I shouldn't have to pretend that *I* believe in God, that's all, and I'm not going to say the Pledge of Allegiance or

144

sing that last verse of *The Star Spangled Banner*. Not ever!"

Frank shrugged. "Okay, don't. Does that settle it?"

I couldn"t think of an answer for that, because it kind of made sense that if all the others wanted to, they could, and if I didn't want to, I didn't have to. But underneath, I didn't feel good about it and felt that it was wrong to make some people stand apart in an official public ceremony because of private beliefs. But I couldn't understand this too well, and certainly couldn't explain it, so I just said, "Okay," and that was that.

But George Meridel and I hate each other now. We both know it.

I also suffered another defeat at the S.R.C. meeting. I proposed that we start writing a Constitution for the revolution (I had freedom of religion in mind, and hoped I could write that part of it), but Frank said we were in the middle of a revolution and martial law was the only constitution we could have right now. George Meridel said, "What's wrong with the United States Constitution?"

Anyhow, at seven-fifty-five a.m., on go the loud-speakers, out comes the Only Voice with a Smell: "Attention! This is Lieutenant Meridel. It is five minutes to eight. In exactly five minutes, everyone will be in the Quad for morning flag-raising ceremonies," and in case no one heard, he repeated it.

So I got up and went down to watch, but I just stood apart. It made me feel bad. Question: is it sometimes better to be a liar so as not to have to stand apart like that? It really made me feel creepy.

After they sang the National Anthem, we heard Stanley Runk's voice coming down from The Brig: "Oh, say can you see by the dawn's early light, what so *prawouawouoodly* we hail," and I couldn't help but think it was funny, although I didn't much like winding up with Stanley Runk as my only "ally" against the ceremony.

Paul Indian asked me why I bothered bringing a Bible up here if I didn't believe in it, so I told him how my mother insists on my reading a chapter every night just because I *don't* believe in it, and even Paul had to smile at that. Then I got a little peeved and told him I had read many books that I didn't necessarily believe in, and it didn't have much to do with anything, anyhow.

Well, getting back to this lousy day, Frank announced at the S.R.C. meeting following the officers meeting that we all have to begin taking some part in the drilling of the platoons, it is our job to give little talks to boost morale, and to point out the need for pride, and to keep reminding everyone about awards and the possibility of getting raised in rank. He also told us we could inform them that we would have some war games before long, games a lot more exciting than "Capture the Flag." And he said we had to point out that everyone owes some loyalty to the revolution, seeing how far it has gone, and seeing that everyone has in some way helped to make it a success and enjoyed its advantages, such as parties and seeing girls and other things.

I got assigned to talk to Fred Elston's platoon, and I told them more or less what Frank said to tell them.

The drills are short and are just for the sake of order, I would gather. Guys drill for less than an hour and do calisthenics for maybe twenty minutes or a half hour, and then go swimming or something. No more than two platoons drill at once in the meadow, and ordinarily there is only one platoon drilling at a time. It doesn't seem like much of a "training program" so far, and I can't see what it is supposed to serve unless it is order.

Now I come to the "trial" of John Mason. It was scheduled for ten, but didn't begin until nearly eleven. We went over to Low Pines and sat in the office there, with both Frank and Susan behind Mrs. Knute's desk, and I and Paul and Blackridge and Edna Kay and Jean Laughlin, Bernice Royer and Dick Richardson sitting in chairs along the wall and the door, facing the desk. Then, sitting across from one another at the sides of the room, were John Mason and a sort of pretty girl of about fourteen. Her name is Thelma Hogan and she just sat there looking mad all the time, and I don't think it was just Mason she was mad at. She just didn't like the trial itself.

John's case was that Thelma Hogan had been willing, and it wasn't just his fault at all, and I could see the girl hated him for saying that, but I couldn't see from her face whether it would have been a true statement or not. Frank asked her and she said, "If I was willing, do you think I'd have gone and told people what he did?"

"You might have, Thelma, if you were afraid of the consequences." Frank stared at her grimly, like he could dig the truth out of her with his eyes.

"Well, I wasn't willing," she said bitterly, so that I believed her.

John Mason said, "What were you doing with me all alone out there, then?"

She mumbled, "You bastard."

"You went out with him, then?" asked Frank.

"Sure I did," she said. "We took a walk.".

Frank said, "You had no idea that going for a walk

out in the woods that late at night could lead to anything?"

"Look," Thelma told him angrily, "I've gone on walks with guys at night before, but this was the first time I went with a guy like that."

Susan Langer said, "I don't see any need to talk about this so much. We aren't here to decide whether she's lying or not."

Frank said, "She did go out with him into the woods, though."

"I went for a walk in the woods with a guy myself," Susan answered, "and I'm still whole."

Jerome Blackridge said, "Promenade with me, Susie honey."

"Shut up, Jerry," snapped Frank. "Okay, Mason, I guess she's telling the truth."

"Hey," groaned Mason, "what kind of a trial is this? She ain't proved a thing."

"Well," said Frank, "you haven't denied anything either, except you say she was willing."

"Hey, though," Mason groaned some more, "that makes a difference, you know. Listen, you'll have to put fifty guys away if every guy who touches one of these girls gets a sentence. Listen, I don't want to be locked up with those counselors any more. Come on, be sports, you guys. That Taber, he nearly knocked my teeth out once. He was talking too much and I only told him to keep his fly closed for a while, that's all I said, and he slapped me so hard I thought my teeth was orbiting my brain. There ain't any freedom in there. Listen, what I'm saying is this: I'm innocent. See?"

"Oh, shut up," Frank said, and he turned to Thelma. "It's up to you. How do we punish him?"

"Murder him," she said at once.

Frank sat back and sighed and began playing with a

pencil. I noticed that his eyes have begun to blink more, or maybe twitch, but he was really doing a lot of blinking all of a sudden.

John Mason himself just threw his arms up and cocked his head, as if to say that Thelma was hopeless, and then he looked at her like she was a naughty girl and he didn't know what to do about such a naughty girl.

Finally Frank said, "We can't kill him, Thelma."

She said, "The cops would! An eye for an eye, that's what I say."

Frank frowned. "He didn't kill you, did he?"

"Listen," said John Mason, throwing his arms up again, "rape me, Thelma. Rape me. I deserve it."

"Kill him," said Thelma with a hiss. "That's what I want. Kill him or stop asking me what to do with him."

"Wake up," Frank put a kind of blinking glare on her. "We've got to wind up this revolution as cleanly as we can."

"Well, it hasn't been clean," Thelma shot right back at him.

"But most of the guys have!" Frank replied. Then he rubbed his eyes for a minute and went on, "Not all the guys have to be hurt just because one guy lost his head. And not all the girls have to be hurt just because you got hurt. Thelma, I want to be on your side. I know you're right and I want to be on your side. But you have to help a little."

Thelma just blew up. "What do you want me to do?" she yelled. "You want me to say you should put him in the dentention room till the end of the revolution? Kill him! That's what I say. I just want you to kill him!"

Frank looked like for once he had nothing to say.

Soon Susan Langer said, "We can't do that, Thelma."

Frank shook his head. "Okay, well, I'm going to adjourn this session, Thelma, and I want you to think it over carefully. I'll call another session either tomorrow or the next day. Maybe you'll decide some other punishment will do. Jerry, take Mason back to The Brig."

"I'm telling you," said Mason, "I don't want to go back in there. I got no friends in there. Listen, put me in with the girls, see? Put me in with Warren, then, but let me stay over here."

"Shut up," Frank said, very angry.

So Jerome Blackridge tied up Mason's hands behind him again, and they took him back to High Pines.

Afterward I asked Frank if Mr. Warren was in the Low Pines detention room, but Frank just said, "We shift him around when we have business with him," and then he began talking with Susan Langer.

Some of the insignia came out today. There is a girls' craft cabin at Low Pines and so there was no problem in getting hold of cloth and thread and stuff, and the girls working on the insignia got out the designs which were okayed early today, I guess, and they have finished sewing some of the insignia already. The highest officers, including me, are now wearing insignia. The insignia for general is a star in a circle sewed with gold thread, the circle being white. The insignia for colonel is a star sewed with blue thread. The insignia for me, Manuel Rivaz and Edna Kay (major) is a star sewed with red thread (and I complained about this because a red star, as I would think anyone knows, is a famous Communist symbol, and I could see plenty of cracks coming my way from George Meridel about me wearing a red star, so Frank said they would change it to some other color later). The insignia for captain is a square sewed with brown thread, but these have not been made yet. I had to make posters with these insignia, with my committee, and get them posted around so people will recognize them.

So now I have a red star on my T-shirt, and George Meridel behind me, and I guess I better start reading Marx all over again. Children of the world, unite! Brick the brains that blind you!

I also took the time to make up some notices today for every cabin—which quoted Thomas Jefferson on the subject of religious freedom—and I pointed out that the revolution has got to be a revolution that doesn't fight the American way of life, no matter what, and therefore everyone was free, and if anyone just didn't happen to believe in God, then he didn't have to say the Pledge of Allegiance, either, or even sing the last verse of the National Anthem. George Meridel saw one and nearly shed his skin, which if he had he would have right away saluted it and Pledged his Allegiance to it, since it's only his skin which really interests him, anyhow. I hear he just ripped my notice down like the words were staring at him stark naked or something, and he ran off double time to General Frank and put it in front of the Presence, and so I was called into it, and Frank told me: "George is right, for this reason: if we make a law in the S.R.C., then the main thing about that law is people have got to keep it. We voted on that law, and you can't go changing it by yourself. If there is a law which says everyone has got to do something, then that doesn't mean they have got to do it only if they want to. You understand?"

"Well," I said, "it's an evil law, since it is un-American."

"Are you nuts?" asked George Meridel, and I had to think about it seriously, coming from him, since he is

151

an expert on nuttiness. "You're talking about the Pledge of Allegiance and the National Anthem. How could they be un-American? Do you think every school in the country is un-American? Do you think the Congress is un-American? You, you're nuts, that's what you are. He's nuts, General Reilley, and he's a Red, too."

"You better shut up," I told Meridel.

"Why should I?" Meridel said. "You, you Red skeleton, you spy, you un-American, are you going to charge me a nickel if I don't? Why had I better shut up?"

"Because I'm a major," I told him, "and I'm ordering you to shut up."

"Well," Meridel took just a moment to size me up, "I'm going to knock you down so hard you'll fall all the way to private."

I was just boiling and didn't know what else to do, so I cried, "Meridel! Attention!"

"Both of you guys shut up," Frank told us.

"I'm a major," I said, "and I ordered him to shut up and he refused to obey my order. Arrest him!"

Frank said, "Shut up!"

So we shut up.

Then Frank looked at me long and hard and I got very uncomfortable. He looked like he was going to speak softly, because his eyes were sad-looking, but his voice was just plain cold. "This morning we voted to have a flag-raising ceremony, after listening to your objections. The vote remained nine to one in favor of it. The purpose of this rule is to create order. Win, remove all the posters you put up. Do it fast."

George said, "And since it's a law, he has to say the Pledge of Allegiance, too."

"That's enough," said Frank, still looking at me with sad eyes, but speaking with his cold voice.

"I'm not saying the Pledge of Allegiance," I said.

"That's enough, enough!" cried Frank. "You understand? I don't want any more trouble over this or I'll put you both in The Brig? You understand?"

Meridel saluted.

So I got mad and hurried out of there, and left George and Frank talking together. I had to go to all the cabins and take down my notices and I was so furious I didn't know what to do, so I went and stuffed the notices under George's covers on his bed but that didn't really help me feel better, either.

I'm still mad. What's the good of thinking, what's the good of trying to get knowledge, when knowledge only hurts. Maybe I'll just start a counterrevolution somehow, and if I was running this revolution, it would be different. We would make the revolution *for* something instead of just against things, and then maybe it wouldn't be quite so bad, and if you're really fighting for something, maybe people would even sympathize more with us after the revolution is over. So long as nobody got hurt, that is. But of course, it wouldn't do any good to start a counterrevolution, because nobody even understands about things, they don't understand about Thomas Jefferson, they don't understand about religion, they don't understand about freedom, they only understand fun.

So maybe I'll quit and just go back to chasing butterflies. Then they would watch me, of course, like they watch Don Egriss, because they wouldn't trust me. But maybe I would feel more free that way.

JUNE 14

It's not even lunch time yet, although somehow it seems later, and since I am feeling bad and have nothing to do, I am writing now.

Well, to begin at the beginning, it was real early this morning and I couldn't sleep. I don't know why. I guess it was four o'clock or so, and I took out my flashlight and decided to go over these ten letters I had left from yesterday's outgoing letters, and while I was reading I heard something and got out of bed to see what it was.

At first I couldn't see, but then I could tell from the way he walked that it was Don Egriss, so I ran quietly up to him.

"I'm going out," he told me.

I said, "Which way?"

"Up through the meadow and out of the woods."

"They have guards all around. You better be careful."

He said, "I can handle Reilley's guards."

"I think you can get out by going along by this little pond way down the river, there are some caves there that smell like dead rats or something. I saw a path up along there the other day, and I didn't see any guards."

"Thanks, kid," he nodded.

"I guess you better try that."

"Thanks."

I followed him a little way, then said, "Don, you know something?"

"Yeah?"

"When you saved me, when I was drowning?"

"Yeah?"

"I lied about that. I was really drowning."

"Who you trying to kid, boy? Listen, you better get on back."

"You really saved my life."

"Cut it out. And keep your voice down, will you?"

"Are you going to squeal on us?"

"I don't know."

"Maybe you better."

He looked at me a time, then looked around. "Well, so long, kid."

"So long, Don."

Then he went off and I went back to the cabin and thought about Don for a while, then worked on the letters for a while and finally did get back to sleep, and I dreamed that I got put in The Brig and that my father was in The Brig with me, and he was going to beat me, he had his belt off, but he just kept shouting at me and shouting at me and never did get around to beating me.

After I woke up I found out that Don didn't get far. I had just started out for the Administration Building for the morning S.R.C. meeting when I ran into Frank, and he walked with me, saying, "Another guy tried to get out last night, Win."

I asked, "What did you do to him?"

"To who?" Frank asked without looking at me. I glanced at him and saw his eyes were blinking that crazy way again, like he had a twitch. "He's in The Brig, of course."

I was feeling very gloomy.

"You don't seem very surprised, Win. But then, you already know it was Don Egriss, don't you?"

I just muttered, "I like Don Egriss."

Frank nodded grimly. "I know that. Why didn't you report to us he was trying to get out?"

There was that business about informing again. It would have been terrible to sneak on Frank to Mr. Warren, but it was fine for me to sneak on Don Egriss, who was my friend, to Frank. I sure don't understand how this squealing code works. So I just said, "I couldn't squeal on Don. He's my friend."

We had come up to the Administration Building and stood there with Jerome Blackridge, who said, "You helped him, didn't you, Weyn?"

"What do you mean?" I asked.

Frank said, "Egriss has been watched ever since the revolution began. Didn't you know that? Do you think we stopped watching him just because the lights went out?" I stared at Frank and his twitching eyes and I don't know why, but all of a sudden I began to be scared of him. I just suddenly felt like Frank Reilley had no feelings, no real feelings at all, and that explained why he could look one way and then another and say one thing is right now and say it is wrong next time. I shuddered, and maybe he saw I was kind of scared, because he began to glare at me. "Win, we only watched him harder when the lights went out. We watched him harder."

"But why didn't you stop him before he tried to leave, then?" I asked.

"That's right," grinned Blackridge, "you know we didn't stop him before that, don't you? Because you saw him off, didn't you? Sometimes if you're patient, you get two mice in one trap. That's knowledge, kid, and it don't come out of books," and Blackridge tapped his head like he thought something was in it.

I said, "I just woke up and saw him going."

"That was about four o'clock this morning," said Blackridge. "What were you doing up at four o'clock?"

"I was going over some letters."

"Yeah?" said Frank. He nodded to Susan Langer, who was just coming up. Paul Indian was coming down another path and it was crazy to see kids moving around in the morning sun like that, and feel the breeze and see the leaves waving, and to be involved in such a crazy situation. I was feeling sick. "Well, that was very loyal of you, Win. But by not reporting Egriss, you betrayed the revolution. You were afraid to get one guy into trouble, so you were willing to let us all get into trouble."

"It wasn't any different," I said, "than not reporting you to Mr. Warren right when you first talked about having a revolution, because then I'd have got a couple guys into trouble, but now everyone is in trouble."

Frank looked at me like I had hit him, he really did. I didn't mean to say anything that would upset him so much. "What the hell kind of remark is that?" he spat at me, twitching double time, his fists all clenched.

"Well hell," good old Manuel Rivaz had got there and was standing by Blackridge, "leave the kid alone. What did he do, say goodbye to a pal? If it was my pal, I'd have said goodbye, too. Anyhow, he couldn't have stopped Egriss. This kid, he's maybe thirteen and he looks nine. Egriss is sixteen and could pass for twenty. The kid couldn't have done anything, could he?"

Paul Indian didn't understand what was happening at all. He said, "What did he do?"

Frank said nastily, "He could have reported him, that's what he could have done."

Then everybody was very still, mostly because Frank was looking like he couldn't make up his mind what to do with his face. He was just on fire with rage and I was still feeling scared of him, and scared because I figured he had it in for me as a counterrevolutionary.

Then I said something else which, once I had said it, I decided was wrong, which was, "Can I visit him?"

"Who?" Frank asked, "Egriss?"

I was regretting I had asked that.

Frank clacked his tongue but then thought it over and said, "Why do you want to visit him?"

"He's my friend, that's all."

Frank nodded. I was surprised. He said, "Okay. Win, you ought to be in The Brig yourself. You better know that."

I just stared at the ground.

"You can visit him for half an hour," Frank told me. "Come on in," and I followed everyone into the Administration Building and everyone sort of watched me and kept still, and it seemed like I was at my own funeral. Frank gave me a note to give Dick Richardson, saying I could visit Don. I couldn't see why he did it, but I wasn't going to stay around wondering about it, and I really hurried out of the Administration Building.

First I went to the mess hall and got some apples for the people in The Brig, and then I went down there, even though I was afraid of having to see Mr. Warren or anyone. But when Dick Richardson unlocked The Brig for me, and I went in, the first thing I saw was that there were only three guys in there: John Mason, Stanley Runk and Don Egriss.

Don said, "What did you do?"

I told him I had come to visit him and asked where everyone was.

"Hey!" cried John Mason, standing up on his bunk. "There's the big officer, he's come to torture me, to beat me. He's trying me, that big officer is. He's come to hang me. Help! Help! Let me out of here!"

Stanley Runk laughed. Mason gave his baboon laugh.

I asked where everyone was again, and Don said he believed everyone had been moved over to Low Pines. They were all taken out early in the morning, except for Mr. Warren, who was supposed to be over there already and, according to John Mason, he was just kept over at Low Pines all the time. I wondered why everyone was over at Low Pines, so I went to ask Richardson through the window.

"Hell," said Richardson. "You got a general in there with you. Ask him."

"Lay off, Richardson," Stanley jumped up and ran to the window and looked out with me. "I'm not going to be in here forever. You better remember that."

Richardson shrugged and said, "Maybe Reilley figures this Brig is going to be getting fuller. How do I know?"

So I went back and sat beside Don Egriss on his bunk.

Stanley came over and bent down and peered right into my face and said, "Major Weyn, sir, hey, Major Weyn, sir, hey you, Major Weyn, sir," and he kept saluting and saying, "Major Weyn," over and over, until he just got tired of it, I guess.

Don Egriss told me not to pay any attention to the Punk, and John Mason gave us another baboon laugh. What a place. I sure felt sorry for Don, having to stay in there with those two guys. But I gave them all some apples, and when he got an apple, Mason not only did another baboon laugh, he began to scratch under his arms and jump all over his bunk in gratitude. Somehow, he seemed to do it too well.

"Well," I sat next to Don, "I guess you won't have to be in here too long. The revolution can't go on much longer."

"What made you come to visit me?" he asked.

"I don't know." I began to eat an apple myself. "I just did." Then I told Don how I was having trouble with the S.R.C., because of the Pledge of Allegiance and the last verse of the National Anthem, and Don found that funny, which surprised me, and he laughed.

"You sure got troubles," he said.

"Hey," said John Mason, "I want you to thank General Reilley for taking old Taber out of here. I want you to tell him I've reformed. I'm going straight from now on. Honest. Will you tell him that?"

"Listen, Major Weyn," said Stanley Runk, coming over again, "sir, will you do me a favor? When they hang Mason, let me pull the rope free. Listen, no kidding, do me a favor. Will you do me one little favor? Get me my knife. Listen, Major, sir, get me my knife, see? I'll make you a colonel. I'll make you a general. You get me my knife and I'm going to make you President. What do you say?"

I told Stanley I couldn't do that, but that he shouldn't worry because the revolution couldn't last much longer and he'd be out soon.

"What do you know about politics, you little fink," he sneered at me, "you little crap-making machine. What a major. What an army that Reilley's got. Winnie Pooh, get me my knife. Do me that one favor, will you? I'll give you two dollars if you get me my knife."

I said, "I can't do that."

"What's the matter, you don't like me?" Stanley growled. "You don't like me, Major, sir? Hey, why don't I knock your eyeballs back into your brain, Major, so you could always see what you was thinking?"

And then, for a while, Mason would say one thing and Runk another and they kept after me until I could see clear enough that it was no use trying to visit Don, so I told him I'd try to come again later and I got up.

But just as I got up, John Mason suddenly grabbed me around my throat and held me so tight I started to choke, and he called out to Dick Richardson, "Hey, Richardson! We got a hostage, we got a hostage in here, so you let us out or you got a dead hostage!"

"Let me go!" I tried to say but could only squeal, and I could hardly struggle he held me so tight, and Dick Richardson opened the door and stepped inside with about six or seven guys, but they didn't move, they just stood at the door like they couldn't think what was the right thing to do. Then all at once Don Egriss must have got behind Mason and pulled him off me, because I fell down and then I was being dragged right out of The Brig by Dick Richardson and Al Santangelo and then I was outside, just gasping to get my breath back, and shaking because I was scared.

And while I sat on the ground like that, Don Egriss came to the window and held to the bars there and he shouted, "You better get me out of here, Richardson, I'm telling you!" He was gulping down his breath just like I was. "You get me out of here because, man, one of these times I'm going to start on one of these guys and not stop."

I wanted to look in the window to see what Mason and Runk were doing, but I was too scared. I was even scared of Don Egriss, the way he was shouting and the things he was saying, and I wanted to cry but was too ashamed and so I got up and went away.

Later, I reported all this to Frank, and I tried to get Frank to let Don out, or at least take him over where the counselors and Mr. Warren are at the girls' camp. Frank told me, "I'll take care of it," without even looking at me, and I knew it was no use talking to him. He had just stopped liking me.

Then Frank said, still not looking at me, "There's a special meeting at twelve noon. Be there."

"That's lunch time," I said.

"Be there," he glared over at me.

JUNE 14

Later

John Mason is dead. Don Egriss killed him, that's what is said. They say Don shot Mason with that revolver Mr. Warren had in his desk, but if he did, how did he get it? I don't know what really happened. But if anyone put that gun in The Brig, I'll bet it was Jerome Blackridge, who maybe did it just for a joke, because he's so evil. But I am not even an officer any more, so I can't simply go to visit Don and ask him what happened.

But I'm glad I'm not on the S.R.C. any more. I'm glad I'm not an officer. I think they will arrest me soon, because now that I'm not an officer I guess I don't have any right not to keep rules, like saying the Pledge of Allegiance, so they will watch me and then accuse me of breaking rules and arrest me.

I don't feel like writing and I *do* feel like writing. I'm sad, so don't want to write, but I'm also mad, and cannot stop being mad, and what I should really do is just try to go home, like Don did, but now that Don is in trouble, I can't think what I should do to help him. But what if he really did kill John Mason?

That twelve o'clock "meeting" was called just for me. The whole S.R.C. marched over to the mess hall where the guys were eating, and I still didn't know what was happening, but it turned out that I was going to become a "public example." They lied about me and didn't give me any chance to say they were lying. They had a girl there and she lied about me. She is one of the girls who worked on the insignia designs, I guess. So first they made everyone quiet and said there was going to be a public court-martial of a traitor. But it was like a floor-show, that trial, like you see in movies and on television as happening in nightclubs, because we were up on the platform and there were all the guys eating stew, and I was being tried, or court-martialed as Frank called it.

First of all it was stated that I had brought a book by Karl Marx to High Pines. Then it was stated that I wrote counterrevolutionary and even Communistic stuff in my diary. Next, George Meridel said that I had tried to keep him from making a rule in favor of people saying the Pledge of Allegiance even before the revolution, when it was to be a rule only for his cabin. Next, Frank said I had tried to keep not only the Pledge of Allegiance, but even the National Anthem (he said "*our* National Anthem") from being sung every morning, and he pointed out that I had lowered the flag when the revolution began even though no one asked me to do it, not mentioning that at least it was the Bear Flag and not the American flag. Then they pointed out I helped Don Egriss to try to betray the revolution (this was true, of course), and then came this other lie about me, which the girl from Low Pines told. She said I had asked for the insignia for major to be a red star, which was the Communist symbol. She said she didn't know it was a Communist symbol, and so she had agreed to it. This is a lie. I never even *saw* that girl before today, at least I don't remember ever seeing her. I even told Frank myself it was a Communist symbol and I wanted to change it so George Meridel wouldn't make cracks about me. Next it was pointed out that I had refused to join in the flag-raising ceremony.

Frank said all of these activities were counterrevolutionary and subversive, and that the revolution began as a way of having fun and hadn't been prepared to "be confronted with true traitors to us all" (me). No one was supposed to be hurt, Frank said, but there were trouble-makers around and no matter how anyone looked at it, they weren't trying to make an anti-American Communist kind of revolution at High Pines, because Frank wouldn't stand for that and was sure no one else would, either. He said he was disgusted. He really was. He said he was ashamed of me. His voice went all soprano about it. I felt like crying, just like I did before, but I was too scared, like before, and couldn't. Anyhow, it looked like Frank might beat me to it and cry himself, he was so ashamed of me. He made me stand up and he ripped that red star off my T-shirt (and tore a hole in it, too) and now the insignia for major is a red square.

Frank said that because of my high rank and previous service, I would not be put in The Brig unless I continued my subversive activities, but he demoted me in public like that to the rank of an ordinary militiaman and I was appointed to Bob Daly's platoon.

Now I want to write something that surprised me and made me want to cry even more than listening to Frank. Because all of a sudden, after I was demoted, Ham Pumpernil jumped up and tore off his own insignia and he threw it right up on the platform, at Frank's feet. Frank was just shocked and I was scared what he might do to Ham. Ham ran out of the mess hall yelling, "I quit!" I never did have a friend like that, I never did, and I like Ham even better than my brother.

I like Ham and Don and wish they were my brothers, and I wish everyone else up here was just dead.

The really flabbergasting rotten thing is that a lot of guys really do think I'm a traitor now. I don't mean a traitor to the revolution, but a traitor to the whole country. To the President. To America. So I have a lot of enemies now. And then, right after my court-martial, like he wanted to make everyone think of something else, Frank announced that the biggest party of all, with prizes for all kinds of things, like dancing, Indian grip, a lot of nutty things, is going to be held tomorrow night. I hadn't even been dismissed and just stood there while he announced it, right next to him, but I had the feeling I wasn't invited. Everyone applauded, and Frank Reilley does seem in charge of High Pines more than ever. The guys just leave everything to the S.R.C., they don't care to think about anything, so naturally Frank gets stronger and stronger. I think that the more confusing things become, the more easy it is to handle people, and I'm not even sure that Frank Reilley doesn't want things to get so complicated that people will be more and more confused, and have to depend on him.

JUNE 15

I had to drill for nearly two hours this morning and I hated it. The other guys don't even seem to care. Why, they even seem to like drilling, and I don't understand them at all. Why would people like to stand next to other people and be told how to walk and when to take a step? March, march, march. Bob Daly is making it rough on me, too, I think, although the roughest thing is that yesterday I was a major and today I am marching in Lieutenant Bob Daly's platoon.

Paul Indian resigned from the S.R.C. this morning, and I have to admire him for this. Paul and Ham are in other platoons, and that's too bad. They too are both ordinary militiamen now, but Frank was careful to put us all in different platoons.

So we marched. We marched up the meadow, then down the meadow, then across the meadow, then around the meadow. Two hours of left, right, left, right, squad, halt! one, two, look alive, look sharp, forward, ho, hup, hup, in step, count, three, four, halt! One, two, three, four, one, two, three, four, hup, hup, hup, hup! Boy, it sure is good for people, this stuff. Really wonderful training. If this is how they make men, then all I can say is that it's pretty simple to make men and doesn't require much more of God than that to get through kindergarten. Like Bob Daly probably did.

And after lunch, we had calisthenics, and that was also a delight. I can do two whole pushups in a row, but they want me to do ten. They seem to think that if they want me to do ten, ten is how many I can do and I'm lying about the other eight. Tomorrow we are supposed to cut down tree branches and whittle them into poles, and the idea is we have to learn how to fight with these poles, called "lances." Who do they think we are going to fight? Robin Hood?

There are so many things I'm trying to understand. I think and think, but can't understand them. Don Egriss is in The Brig, and they say he killed John Mason. And today they actually buried John Mason. I guess they had to, since he is dead, but I can't see how the revolution can go on like this. Gogo Burns told me it was a very respectable kind of ceremony, and Frank even read from my Bible out there, somewhere toward the place where the river winds back before it shoots on down by the caves. It is all so awful, but the thing I can't understand most of all is myself. I go up and I march after breakfast and do calisthenics after lunch and I take a book and read, and I think about Mama and wonder why I ever had to come up here, and go on reading or thinking about other things. Why don't I just cry, or why don't I just run away? Something is so crazy and awful about these things that I feel almost *empty,* like I don't even care if I go home or not, or say the Pledge of Allegiance or not, I just don't care what happens. Except I wish I hadn't come here, that's what I wish most of all.

I didn't want to go to the party at the mess hall, and so I just read instead. I think Irene Mannering wouldn't care to see me any more, now that I am a militiaman. And I came across this interesting remark in Thoreau, who I like very much because he decided to go to jail instead of pay some taxes when he believed the money was going to be spent in an evil way. He wrote a lot of good things, like this: "Under a government which imprisons any unjustly, the true place for a just man is also a prison." That is quite a statement. So I am wondering if I should ask Frank to put me in The Brig with Don Egriss, because I know that Don didn't do anything evil and, anyhow, he was put in prison just for wanting to go home. I have been thinking about this ever since I read it.

Today the Bear Flag went down (and I was charged with treason for taking down that same flag!) and the Revolution Flag went up. The Revolution Flag is all white, with a yellow star in a yellow circle, which is just like Frank's insignia for general. They made the flag out of real silk which they found somewhere, and I guess it is kind of pretty, but I don't like it anyhow.

JUNE 16

Hup, two, three, four, hup, two, three, four. Left, hup, left, hup, squad, halt! HALT YOU GOD DAMN SON OF A BACKWOODS BITCH WHEN I SAY HALT. YOU STOP RIGHT THERE WHAT'D YOU HAVE FOR A MOTHER, A FUCKING FLEA? First column to the left, march! Second column to the left, march! Third column to the left, march! Fourth column to the left, march! It got to be so I was nearly ready to report Bob Daly to George Meridel for making us go to the left so much. One, two, three, *lunge!* One, two, three, *lunge!* Strike! Strike! Strike! This is lance training. "Kick him in the balls! Kick him in the balls."

I read some more from Thoreau. I read more now, just so I can think about problems and not about the things that happen, themselves. I think I agree with Thoreau where he writes: "I think that we should be men first, and subjects afterward. It is not desirable to cultivate a respect for the law, so much as for the right. The only obligation which I have a right to assume is to do at any time what I think is right." I like that very much because, unless a guy is nuts (like most of the guys up here), it is usually easy to know what is right by other people, and people should do what is right. I guess he is right, too, about going to jail. If that's where the good people are, then that is the place for me. I said this to Paul today, and he didn't like drilling any more than I do, he said, but he didn't think he'd like to be in The Brig, either.

"Stay outside The Brig, then," I answered him, "and keep taking their lessons. You know what they're doing? They're teaching us to act like Jerome Blackridge—to beat people. They're teaching us to be like them, and I guess most of the guys are learning, too."

So I told him I was going to go to The Brig.

Paul said, "How will you do it?"

"I'm going to give Bob Daly a whack with my pole, and if he hasn't reported me for refusing to kick dirty, then he'll be sure to report me for that."

And that is what I am going to do.

JUNE 17

High Pines has a motto now, which is *On Our Terms*.
All the guys are saying it. It was announced over the
loudspeakers this morning, and Frank said the revolu-
tion would continue until we could be sure the majority
of kids would be safe in surrendering—until we could
surrender *On Our Terms*. Also, Frank announced that
Don Egriss leaked out news about the revolution.
Frank said Don had sneaked out and made a trip into
Wellberg some days ago and had squealed, and the
Wellberg people advised him to come back into High
Pines so as no one in camp would be aware that they
were making preparations against us.

"Thanks to this traitor," announced Frank, "the authorities in Wellberg are now thoroughly convinced that
this is no innocent revolution, and that there is no
innocent kid in all High Pines and Low Pines, with the
exception of Don Egriss of course, and possibly one or
two friends of the traitor." Frank said he could have
sympathized with a guy who just had it in for a couple
guys he didn't like, but he asked everyone to think
about whether it was reasonable for Don to try to get
everyone into trouble like that. He also said, "There
will be two minutes of silence at twelve noon for John
Mason," and then he said, "On our terms!" and at last
he went through his notes—you could hear the paper
over the loudspeaker—and said, "Goodbye, then."

I left the mess hall and went to my cabin to stuff some books under my shirt, and before I could finish that, Frank was at it again. This time his voice came from the loudspeaker in the pine trees, by Cabin Nine:

"Today, all drills are doubled. Remember, your effort is an effort not only for yourself, but for all of your friends at High Pines. From now on, awards of money will be offered for outstanding effort. The first militiaman to win the Master Soldier's medal will also win five dollars; the second will win three dollars, and the third two dollars. Help your pals to be prepared for any action which might force us to surrender on their terms. Make High Pines strong under the motto, *On Our Terms,* and remember that our terms are the terms which protect you, and get you home safer and sooner. And now, a special announcement: the traitor, Don Egriss, has confessed that he had two accomplices in his attempts to betray the revolution and all of us. The names of these two will be announced shortly, once they have been locked in The Brig. Do not betray the revolution! Goodbye, then."

I listened to Frank's words and I just shuddered. I was flabbergasted and sat back to think about them. Someone says something, so you listen. It doesn't matter if the guy who says something believes what he says or not, you just listen. Everyone takes what he says seriously, so you take it seriously, too. When I listened to that announcement, I actually wondered how it could be that Don Egriss could have had accomplices, and I wondered who they were, and it took me a couple of minutes just to think that everything Frank was saying was a lie, and that everything Frank says is likely to be a lie, just because there is no *reason* that anyone could think of for Frank to tell so many lies.

Finally, I stuck my diary, my Herodotus and my political-philosophers books under my belt, and only my diary was big enough to make me uncomfortable and have to walk a little funny; and I put my flashlight in my pocket and I went off to drill.

We were drilling with our "lances" for about five minutes before I stepped out of place and went up and tapped Bob Daly on the shoulder with my stick. Well, he turned and looked at me very strangely for ten or fifteen seconds, so I tapped him again, a little hard.

He winced and hit my stick away and said, "What are you doing, for Christ's sake!" Then he turned away disgustedly.

So I brought back my pole and gave him a real whack across the shoulders, and he was so surprised he fell down. He got up furiously and grabbed my stick and was about to let me have it, but he suddenly just threw it away and shouted: "Counterrevolutionary!" in my face, and then he told me I was going straight to General Reilley. So he left the platoon in charge of another kid and I went off with Lieutenant Daly to be reported.

Frank was taken by surprise to hear I had hit Bob Daly with my stick, and he laughed, and then he said, "I didn't figure you for a fighter, Win." I told him, "I don't like my platoon leader." Bob Daly, bending his head down, said, "He hit me right on the back of my head, look, look! I even got a bump," but no one could see a bump and I don't think I hit his head, anyhow, and Frank laughed and pushed Daly's head away. Then he sent for Jerome Blackridge and I wondered if I was going to be beaten instead of put in The Brig. Frank dismissed Bob Daly, and I wondered if I would be beaten right there, in Frank's office, and while I worried, George Meridel trotted in and laughed to hear

I was in trouble. "So now you're going to The Brig," he laughed, looking almost friendly, like I had arranged the whole thing as a favor to him, and I felt good, being able to cheer everybody up the way I was doing. Finally Blackridge came and Frank, still chuckling, said, "Take him on down to The Brig. You can spend the night there, Win. Maybe you'll cool off by tomorrow."

So I was only going to get one day in The Brig for hitting Bob Daly. It was looking like I'd have to hit General Reilley himself with my lance. And then, before Blackridge took me away, Frank said, "Take it easy, Jerry. You understand?" I guess by that he meant I was even to be treated okay. Frank sure is hard to understand. I thought he hated me when he did that to me at lunch, court-martialing me in public, but here he was just laughing and saying I should be treated okay and giving me a very light sentence.

Well, no one seemed to notice how healthy I had become in the chest, but of course I was keeping my arms crossed ever since I whacked Bob Daly. So I got myself, my big diary and my little books and even my flashlight into The Brig.

Don Egriss and Stanley Runk were playing a game of gin rummy when I was let in. They were interested to see me there and Don grinned and said, "I heard they drummed you out, kid. Who'd you kill?"

Well, I just took out my books and set them on a bunk and I stood looking at Don, sitting there grinning for a couple seconds, and then suddenly, I can't explain it at all, I just lost my sense of everything, I just stopped thinking and all my unhappy feelings just jumped out of my stomach and went shooting through my throat and it was worse than fainting, even, because I broke up and started to cry. I sat down by my books, looking at Don, and I cried. I bawled. I just kept looking at him and I saw someone look through the window, grinning at me, but I couldn't see who it was through my tears. Don Egriss came over and sat beside me and looked like he didn't know what to do, and even Stanley Runk seemed to be embarrassed, but there was nothing I could do, I couldn't stop, and I went on crying. Don Egriss put his arm around me and so I got even more unhappy and cried harder and Don just held me in his arms and patted me and tried to soothe me, but nothing could stop me, I felt awful, and it was a long time before I could even say, "Why did you do that? What did you do that for?" Don just kept trying to comfort me with crazy words, like he was Mama or something, and I don't know why but I started to love Don all of a sudden, and yet I felt almost like I hated him because of what he did; I was so mixed up that I guess the only thing I could do was cry.

I kept my eyes closed and said, "Frank is saying terrible things about you."

"Sure," he told me, and he patted my back again, like he had to sympathize with me because Frank had said bad things about him, "sure, I know. I hear them dumb announcements."

"I don't believe them," I told him, wanting him to understand this, and he patted my leg and said:

"I know. I know you don't."

"What happened to make you do that, Don?" I asked him, still not looking at him and I just pushed my eyes into his chest so I wouldn't have to open them, and he kept his arms around me and just said:

"It don't matter now, Win. It really don't matter now. Listen, why did they put you in here?"

But I couldn't talk for a while, I had to do a lot of sniffling and finally I got my eyes clear and found I could talk better, so I told him how I decided to hit Bob Daly and how Bob Daly just didn't seem able to figure what it was all about until I hit him so hard he fell down. Don got a good laugh out of that. Then I nearly had to start crying again, for no reason except it felt like I hadn't finished, but I stopped myself and told him instead about the court-martial. Don just looked bewildered. Then I asked him again what had happened, but he told me it was true, he had actually got hold of the gun and shot John Mason, but it had been in a fight. They took Stanley out of The Brig for no reason at all so far as anyone including Stanley could tell (they just took him for a walk), and then they came and took Mason out for a while, but where they took him Don doesn't know, though they brought Mason back pretty soon. And not long after that, Mason picked a fight with Don—even though he knew Don could beat him up. He called Don bad names, he said it was Don who'd attacked a girl in the woods and he wanted to know why Don had blamed it on him. Don finally told him to shut up or he would knock his head off. But Mason had Stanley's knife, and it was obvious he had egged Don into fighting just so that Don would lunge at him, because Don almost ran straight into the knife and the fight was very hard, but Don finally managed to hit the knife out of Mason's hand and he was going to slap Mason around a little more when someone called through the window, "Hey you! Egriss!" And Don looked over and saw a gun was thrown through the window and it fell on a bunk and John Mason just burst out from under Don and threw himself across the bunk and got the gun and Don leaped on top of Mason and they fought harder, and Don said it was only then that he knew he was fighting for his life, that the whole thing might have been arranged for a game or out of hate of him or because of almost anything, but he knew he was fighting for his life. They went on fighting until all of a sudden Don was holding the gun against Mason and he pulled the trigger and shot John Mason. Then Don felt like he went nutty for awhile, he went to the window and began to point the gun everywhere, shouting and pulling the trigger. But there had been only the one bullet in the gun, and a whole bunch of guys came pouring into The Brig and they got John Mason out of there. Don didn't know if Mason was dead or not, he had felt so sick for a long while that he only shouted and hit the wall and he said he'd done some crying himself, and then for a long while Don didn't talk and we just sat there. Stanley Runk went on playing solitaire.

Then I said that the whole thing didn't make sense, it was all just crazy, so Stanley Runk flipped all his cards across the bunk and he lay back with his arms under his head, saying, "You guys don't understand Reilley at all. Me, I can see him like nothing was covering his insides. If you want to know what it's all about, Egriss, you should ask me. I got brains. Runk has brains, men, only nobody uses them. Hey, Winnie Pooh, they ought to make me chairman of the propaganda committee." I guess I didn't feel like smiling or anything, so Stanley went on, "It's simple. Reilley didn't care which one of you got killed. That's all. I'll tell you something else. It's all going to happen again." We didn't understand that a bit, but Stanley said, "Sure, because he only wants one of us left, so there's only one of us to blame for everything," and he leered at us for a while, like he didn't really trust us, and he said, "one of us to blame for the girl, for being a traitor, for killing, for starting the whole thing, and he's got his little lavender eyes on me. Only don't worry, men, I'll get Reilley. I'll get Reilley, all right. I'll get him," and he closed his eyes and looked like he was already getting Frank in his mind.

Finally I said, "I think it was Blackridge who put that gun in here and gave Mason that knife. I just don't see how Frank could be that evil."

But no one had anything to say to that. After a time, I asked Don, "What will they do to you?"

"Who?" he asked, "Reilley?"

"No. I mean after."

Don shrugged. "I been wondering."

I sat next to Don, making myself not cry, feeling numb and finally I asked, "What is this dumb revolution about, anyhow?"

"The only thing you need to know," said Stanley, his eyes still shut, "is that Reilley wants a *real* revolution. He's going to get it, too. But me, I'm getting out of here before Reilley thinks. He's got uncouth plans for us, Egriss, but I'm getting out of here. I am, man. If it was me who got hold of that knife, I wouldn't have stopped to fight with you, Egriss. If I'd had that gun, I wouldn't have stopped to shoot John Mason. I'd have gone straight to the General. The Punk's got tools to think with, Winnie Pooh. Stick around. The show ain't over." Then he closed his mouth as well as his eyes, and I couldn't think what to say.

So I asked Don about his accomplices, and he grimaced and said, "Are you kidding?" I told him I didn't really believe he had told anyone about the revolution anyhow, and I knew if he had gone out of the camp he would never have returned, and I showed him some places in my diary where I didn't believe Frank, and told Don I was sorry to have even asked that question. "Hey," he said, looking at this diary, "that's a big book. You sure got to write a lot to keep a book like that going." "My Uncle Giles gave it to me for my birthday," I told him, "just before I came to camp." Don grinned a bit and said, "Happy birthday," his eyes down on my book.

Later tonight, after dinner (they bring plates down from the mess hall), we had a very interesting conversation. I said, "It's too bad if this revolution has to keep going, at least it could fight for something good and be a good revolution instead of a bad revolution."

We were lying in the dark, speaking very softly, while Stanley Runk was snoring. Stanley has a peculiar snore, which comes in short little spurts, like a clock which is a little haywire ticking not quite evenly and too loudly, so you get used to it that way and pretty soon don't hear it at all. He's snoring again right now while I write.

Don thought it over and said, "How could this stupid revolution help people?"

"I only mean that maybe we would be treated better after the revolution if we try to get some good things, some *ideals,* into the revolution."

"So what would you fight for?"

"Well, we could fight for religious freedom, for example."

Don laughed so suddenly he nearly woke Stanley up, but Stanley turned over and then began snoring again.

"Well," I thought about it and saw how Don might suspect I was being selfish about that ideal, "then there is racial prejudice. What do you think about that? There are some states in the United States, I guess, where we couldn't even be at a summer camp together like this."

"Couldn't even be in the same Brig, huh?" chuckled Don.

"You know what I mean."

"Yeah," he seemed to be a little peeved and went on, "well, this ain't those states, kid. This is a dumb little revolution, and revolutions aren't good, they're bad, and you can't make something bad turn into something good the way you want to. You, you want to take a pie made out of mud and call it a real pie just because you spread it over with whipped cream. Fancy words."

So I took out my political-philosophers book and my flashlight and looked up this certain passage I had read through, and I read the words out loud to Don: "What country can preserve its liberties if its rulers are not warned from time to time that this people preserve the spirit of resistance?" And it goes on to say: "Let them take arms." I explained that this was what Thomas Jefferson himself wrote, when there had been some kind of rebellion against the government somewhere, I think in Massachusetts, and Jefferson wrote: "God forbid we should ever be twenty years without such a rebellion."

Don thought about it but only got irritated and said, "Okay, maybe Reilley is another Jefferson, if they both like revolutions so much."

"But Frank's revolution doesn't have ideals."

After we talked about it awhile, Don said that, so long as no one could actually stop the revolution, he would admit it would be better to fight for something good than for nothing at all. Then he said, "Who do we fight? Runk?"

"I don't know. But there are just things somebody ought to fight, and I'm going to tell my Uncle Giles about them, if they don't send me to reform school, and maybe he will tell me how to fight them, and then I'll tell you what he says, if they don't send you to reform school. But wouldn't it be good if we could get all the guys in the revolution to fight against those things?"

Don waited a minute, then only said, "Hey, you go to sleep, Win. You're nuts."

So I went on thinking about things, and it was quite a while later, when everything was dead still except for some crickets way down by the river and one bullfrog, that Don said, "Say, kid? I didn't mean you're nuts, Win. That's one thing you ain't." I didn't know what to say, so he said, "You hear me?" I said, "Thank you," very surprised to have him say that to me, since I never did think he had meant it, but I guess he worried I took it seriously.

JUNE 18

This morning, early, Don and I both woke up, so we talked again. "Me," Don said, "I just don't want to fight anything, for or against. I don't want trouble. Negroes got enough troubles as it is, and you have to be a Negro to know it. Anyhow, too many Negroes are dumb."

I was shocked. I said, "That's an awful thing to say."

"Hell, it's true! My father is dumb and so is my mother. They wouldn't understand you any more than I do. Hell, it was only two hundred years ago they dragged us out of Africa. Me, I'm glad, of course. I can't see myself shooting poison darts at great white hunters or dressing in leopard skins, or drinking banana juice all day, to say nothing of goat's milk and piss. But the way I figure it, maybe that's why my father and mother are more dumb than your father and mother."

I told him, "My father is dumb, too. He's a bill-collector."

Don only said, "What's so dumb about collecting money?"

"And I'm dumb, too, because I collected money for the revolution. Don't tell me *that* wasn't dumb!"

He grinned. "You take after the old man, huh? Listen, kid, you're smart."

"And a long time ago, and even today, and always, I guess, there have been plenty of great men in Africa, and they're plenty smart. Don't you ever read any newspapers?"

"The hell with that. The Bible itself shows how Negroes were slaves from the beginning. What's so smart about that?"

"That's not true, because some Negroes were slaves, maybe, but their masters were Negroes too, weren't they? And they built these great temples and made up a calendar even better than the Greek calendar, and they built cities and palaces and moved the whole Nile River, and they built the pyramids and the sphinxes, and they had writing and there were great kings like Sesostris, and philosophers, and it was the greatest civilization in the whole world. And underneath Egypt there was Ethiopia, and that was supposed to be so powerful that not even Cambyses could beat it, so why say Negroes didn't even have a history?"

"Man, are you saying the Egyptians were colored?"

"Don't you even know that? That's what Herodotus says," and I leaned over and gave him my Herodotus book, "and he was there, wasn't he?"

He looked at the book and said, "You mean those Pharaohs were black as me?" He began to laugh, seeming to think it was only funny, and he said, "Hey, well what happened to them? Those Egyptians sure aren't Negroes today."

"I think what happened is that later the Persians came in and conquered the whole country and took it over, and I guess they just made it a colony. By the time it was through with being a colony, there weren't many pure Egyptians left. There were mainly just the colonialist Egyptians left. So the Egyptians today would just be descended from those colonizers."

We both thought about that and then Don began to flip through my Herodotus book and said, "Is all that in this book?"

"That book has all kinds of stories about places and kings and battles and things, and Herodotus went to Egypt and other places and found out about those things and wrote about them. It's very interesting."

He looked at a page for a while and said, "Herodotus. What a name. Guess I'll pick it up at the prison library."

"You can have that book, Don."

He looked at it and made his lips sort of pout. "No, it's your book. I'll get one for myself."

"But I want you to take that book as a present."

At last Don said, "Okay," and he just kept it beside him.

Then Stanley Runk began to snore louder, and all at once Stanley woke up and shook his head and rubbed his eyes and he sat up and said, "What are you doing, Egriss? Reading?"

"Maybe it's kicks, Runk," Don picked up the book. "Why don't you try it?"

That was funny, so Stanley laughed at it, and then he stood up on his bunk and began to hit the bars at the window with his fists and he kicked the wall with his feet and he started to shout: "Breakfast! Breakfast! Breakfast!" I heard some guys outside begin to laugh at Stanley.

After I was let out of The Brig, I went straight to my cabin to hide my diary and political-philosophers book (which I also hide now that it is subversive) and I put my flashlight away and then I went over to the mess hall. But before I could even find Ham or Paul, Dick Richardson found me and he said Frank had ordered me to go straight to the Administration Building after

185

getting out of The Brig, and why hadn't I gone? I said, "No one told me." He said, "Well, I'm telling you now. So get going."

I went to the Administration Building, and there was Frank with Susan Langer, and I was told to sit down. Frank smiled and said, "How did you like The Brig?" I told him it was just fine. "You want to go back?" he asked me, still smiling. I told him I wouldn't be bothered by it. Then he said, "Why did you hit Daly in the first place?" I admitted I just didn't like him very much and said I might hit him again. Frank called me a real hothead but said, "That's okay. I like your spirit. I think you liked it better being a major and chairman of the propaganda committee. Isn't that your trouble?" I told him I was getting as much to eat and it tasted just as bad as an ordinary militiaman, and I had less work to do, too, and it was even better in The Brig, where I had more time to think subversive thoughts and didn't even have to drill. Frank laughed again. "Listen, small fry," he said, getting serious, "you've got to understand that we're in trouble enough without getting involved in anything that even smells of real subversion. Jesus Christ, Win, every kid here would have a little more trouble, and us guys at the top would get life, they'd say we were trying to brainwash all these kids. I can't have that. If I have to go to jail after this thing is over, okay, but I sure don't want to go to jail for being a traitor."

"I'm not a traitor," I cut in.

"I know that," Frank put his hands up like he meant to bless me, "I know you're not"—and I realized he was talking about the revolution, while I was talking about the country—"I'm just touchy on the subject, Win. And for good reason, because it's my job to keep our troubles from getting completely out of hand. Look at it in the face, Win. We've got a murderer on our hands and the guy who got murdered was accused of a crime nearly as bad, and half the kids here could maybe stand accused of the same, and we've had to censor mail, we've just got too many troubles to add even a touch of Communism to the heap."

"Well, Don Egriss is no murderer," I told Frank.

Frank got mad. He got so mad he clapped his hands together and snapped, "He killed a guy! They'll call it murder."

"Because someone threw a gun in to him and he had to protect himself," I said, "that's what happened."

"All right!" Frank scowled at me a moment, then glanced at Susan Langer.

I looked at Susan and thought she was going to say something, but she only looked down at the floor. I saw she was unhappy and had the feeling that Frank was controlling her in some way and maybe she would be saying some of the things I was saying, and would try to end the revolution, except for Frank and a couple guys like Blackridge and Richardson, maybe, or Rivaz, since Blackridge himself was in trouble.

"All right," Frank wiped his scowl away with his hand and began to blink again, like he was doing a few days ago. "You think I don't know that? You think I haven't been figuring that out? That's what Susan and I have been talking about. Well, we know who did it, too, and so far as we're concerned, he's equally responsible."

"Who?"

"Blackridge, that's who," said Frank, "because he's the only guy outside of you and me who knew where to find that revolver, and you were being court-martialed, and it wasn't me—because I was there."

"I figured it was Blackridge, too," I said.

"Sure. Well, don't worry, we're taking care of him right now, right this minute. What do you think of that?"

I was flabbergasted. "Are you arresting Blackridge?"

"That's exactly what we're doing. What he did was to try to stir up the worst kind of trouble. Why? Maybe just to see a good fight, to get a thrill. Who knows? I don't care, but I do know that trouble like that is counterrevolutionary."

"You were right the first time," Susan Langer said very moodily, though I couldn't tell if she was angry or just impatient. "It was murder."

"Okay," said Frank. "Win, the thing is, I've been doing a little investigating since we court-martialed you and I found out it was George Meridel who put that girl up to saying you asked to have a red star for the major insignia. Now she admits it isn't true that you asked for it, but what could I do? She told me that and I blew my top. I had to believe her."

"Well, she was lying," I said, "and you might have just investigated before court-martialing me, not after."

"I blew my top," Frank shook his head and looked very disgusted with himself. "It's my job to worry about things, so it's easy for me to get worried and move too quickly. Look, I've put that girl in detention at Low Pines for betraying an officer of the revolution. And, to tell the whole story, we've got to arrest Meridel, too, on the same charge. After all, he invented the lie. But we don't mean to put up with lies, especially when they make us hurt kids like you, who really helped make the revolution succeed. Win, I called you here to tell you that we're going to make things right with you again." He paused and added, "Major Weyn."

I thought about all that. But it was too much to think about. I figured he was saying that I was going back to being a member of the S.R.C. and chairman of the propaganda committee and major, too, and not only that, but both Jerome Blackridge and George Meridel were to be arrested. The first thing I thought of was that Don Egriss wasn't about to get very good company, but I was also thinking about what I had talked over with Don, how if I could get some *ideals* into the revolution, maybe it could even accomplish something good.

Finally I asked, "What about Don Egriss?"

Frank frowned. "What about him?"

"If Blackridge was to blame, then do you have to go on punishing Don Egriss?"

"What do you expect me to do? He killed a guy. If I let him out, he'll only try to run off again. There's nothing I can do but hold him till the revolution is over, then turn him over to the cops with Blackridge."

I didn't understand. "But you weren't going to turn Mason over to the cops."

"Murder is different. Good God, can't you see that? We have to account for a guy being missing. Mason is dead. We have to account for that. It's different."

I didn't know what to think and told him I had been thinking about the revolution and how, if it had to go on, it might be better if we could get some ideals into it, so the guys would have something to fight for, and I told him there were still some things to fight for in America, so we might actually accomplish something good instead of just doing a lot of things that ended up all bad. Frank said he would like to think about that, he liked the sound of it and I should write out just what I had in mind and he would be thinking about it. Then he said, "You can put up those notices, too, if you want to, about how guys have to say the Pledge of Allegiance only if they believe in God."

"I thought that was against the order of things," I told him.

"God damn it, Win, that's because you acted on your own. Now I'm telling you it's okay. Order comes from the top. Listen, Win," he tossed his pencil on to his desk "I like you. You're a smart kid and we haven't got much in the way of brains in this revolution. Isn't that right, Susie? We're short on brains. I think the revolution needs you. That Meridel, he's a ninny. The only thing he can think of are rules. He wanted to make it a rule to have everyone in both camps memorize the Gettysburg Address. He wanted us to confiscate your Bible and hold twilight services every night. Every night! As if I don't have enough to think about. That's all that guy did, make up rules and submit them. It's not like when you were chairman of the propaganda committee. You did things completely and carefully. Meridel follows orders, but if I don't think of every detail, well, too many things don't get done. Listen, Win. I trust you. We need you. I'm sorry we fouled you up but we'll make it right by you. That's a promise. A Reilley promise. What about it? I'll tell you what else is on my mind. I was going to surprise you at the ceremony, but here it is: I'm making you colonel and Special Adjutant. Win, I couldn't offer you more. It's so close to being General that I'm shoving myself by doing it, you little twerp, but I feel bad for what happened to you. Okay?"

I didn't realize till right then that Frank actually *did* want me back. I thought he was just trying to make up for feeling so guilty about what he did, but now I began to wonder to myself if I wasn't smarter than I thought, and maybe Frank really did need me, although I couldn't think why.

I considered it all and said, "Can I have my old propaganda committee together again?"

"Of course. Indian and Pumpernil were correct to defend you. We'll make it right by them, too. They'll both be captains."

Well, that was a promotion for Ham, so I finally agreed, thinking that with myself and Ham and Paul on the S.R.C., maybe we really could get some ideals into the revolution. Also, maybe I would be able to make things a little easier on Don.

Susan Langer had to go back to Low Pines, and she left as moodily as she had seemed all the while she stayed. I think she isn't happy but doesn't know what to do, and is probably afraid of being arrested herself. Maybe she's obeying Frank because of reasons like my own, so that she can use her rank to at least make things as easy as possible over at the girls' camp.

After she went, Frank leaned back in his chair and stared at me awhile. I thought he was maybe changing his mind about the whole thing, his face was so dark, but then he smiled and just said, "Hell, Win, you're the most midgety colonel I ever saw. Colonel Weyn. So you want to get some ideals into the revolution?"

I told him it would be good for morale, and if we could accomplish something good, just anything, then maybe people would have at least a little bit of sympathy for us after the revolution.

"What kind of ideals?" he asked.

I talked about Negroes and how they and some other races still have things pretty bad, and then I spoke of freedom of religion and described how only people

191

born strong or rich were lucky and could compete without any disadvantages these days.

Frank squinted and became thoughtful. "Are you sure that isn't a Communist way of thinking?"

I said I didn't know what kind of thinking it was, but mostly I read Thomas Jefferson and Thoreau and John Stuart Mill.

"So you think the whole country ought to have another revolution, is that it?"

That question caught me by surprise, I certainly didn't mean to say that. Thinking about it, I said, "I just meant we should make the revolution fight for some good things."

Frank nodded. "Yeah, but if the revolution had to go on and if it got bigger instead of smaller, if people began to like it instead of dislike it, then you think those things are really important, is that right?"

It felt funny to have him ask me such a question. After all, Frank is a straight-A student, I am told, and though I get good grades, too, he is older than me and why should he ask me what is important? I said, "They are just things I mean to fight for, myself."

"Okay," and then Frank dismissed me kind of suddenly.

So this revolution just gets more and more bewildering, no kidding. Frank is the moodiest guy in the world. But here I am, Colonel Winston Weyn, chairman of the propaganda committee, Special Adjutant to the Supreme Commander, and as such I told Frank that what we should do is not change the Pledge of Allegiance rule, because it is orderly and instructive to have a flag-raising ceremony, but to make it clear that guys don't *have* to attend the ceremony, and then to take out the words "under God" so that the whole revolutionary government could stay free of religion, which is not a matter for governments to decree, as Thomas Jefferson has said. Frank was pleased by the idea, but said I should take great care to explain just why those words were being removed from the Pledge of Allegiance. He also asked me if I had got to the mail yet, and said, "Meridel is a slow reader." I told him I had a big stack of letters to go over and Frank told me to be sure and be at the lunch meeting at the mess hall and at the S.R.C. meeting at three o'clock. I had gone to him to tell him I wanted a note to get Ham and Paul away from their platoons, and Frank gave me the note.

After I found them, we walked over to The Brig just to see if Blackridge and Meridel were really in there, and Paul said, "I can't understand how things keep going back and forth like this," but Ham said, "You can't stop a born leader. You try to push them down and they only spring up that much higher." What a jerk! So when we got over to The Brig and saw Dick Richardson, wearing the insignia of major, he saluted me and we all got mixed up with salutes for a minute, so we stopped. Then I looked into the window and saw a kind of blubbery-faced old George Meridel sitting there, and a cursing old Jerome Blackridge shaking his head at a giggling old Punk, but Don was gone.

"Where's Don Egriss?" I asked, feeling scared.

"Oh," said Richardson, "General Reilley and Major Rivaz, they took him over to Low Pines."

"Why?" I asked.

"To give evidence in that trial over there, of course."

I asked when Don would be back, not understanding what Richardson meant about the trial.

"Jesus, don't ask me, Colonel," Richardson shrugged, smirking. "I'm just a major."

So Paul and Ham and I went away and Jerome Blackridge came to the window to shout curses at us as we went.

Naturally, I was mad and scared about Don being taken to Low Pines. They took Mr. Warren and the counselors and cooks over there, and none of us have even seen them since. I got the idea that maybe Frank was trying to keep Don away from me, since I was Don's friend and might try to use my rank to help him. And it made me mad, too, that I could be a colonel and what Frank calls Special Adjutant, and not even know when a prisoner, who is a friend of mine, is being moved.

Frank didn't get back until lunch time, when we had the ceremony which made me a colonel, and both Ham and Paul captains, and I was given a Hero of the Revolution Medal made of blue cloth with a yellow star in a yellow circle sewed on to it. Also, Dick Richardson was officially promoted to major and Frank had everyone give three cheers for us, and then three more cheers for "the yellow and white." It was all kind of embarrassing, but pretty funny, too, and the kids got a sort of a kick out of all this military-type stuff. So I was out of disgrace and now it is George Meridel and Jerome Blackridge they are saying bad things about.

Frankly, none of this made me feel better at all, so afterwards I asked Frank why Don had to go to Low Pines and Frank said, "The trial isn't over yet and Don became a part of it when he shot John Mason."

"What trial?" I asked.

"Mason's trial, of course."

"But he's dead."

"Tell Thelma Hogan," Frank said with a grin and a chuckle, but he only looked sorrowful. "I think she wants us to execute his ghost, too."

This is what Frank says, and so Don is supposed to stay over at Low Pines until John Mason's trial is over. I don't understand it at all, it sounds like something you would hear in a lunatic asylum. I didn't say anything to Frank, because I was confused and because when Frank gets in a nervous mood, I still feel frightened of him. But I was so mad and feeling so bad for Don to have to talk about killing Mason in a trial like that, well, I didn't know what to do, but I think it was just about then that I began to think about starting a counterrevolution to stop Frank from doing all the crazy things he is doing. Because I think Frank is crazy.

I was thinking about this even before I heard this announcement over the loudspeakers:

"This is General Reilley. At noon, we witnessed proof of the democratic spirit of the Pines Camps revolution: we saw the reinstatement of an officer who had been discredited, and we saw him win promotion as a reward for his having borne dishonor quietly, with the courage we like to see in officers. Colonel Weyn is also to be given a prize of ten dollars, which goes along with the Hero of the Revolution decoration. We salute Colonel Winston Weyn! We salute those who defended him! Earlier, I informed you that the traitor, Egriss, had accomplices in his attempts to betray the revolution and to betray all of you into the hands of those who would harm you. The traitors are Jerome Blackridge, whom we trusted as Chief of the Revolutionary Police, and George Meridel, who through lies sought to gain the position and honors rightfully belonging to the hero, Colonel Winston Weyn. The traitors have been arrested. Traitors are those who seek to help themselves and raise themselves by deceit, who join with the authorities who are not prepared to understand our position and who would harm all of us. Be watchful for traitors! Honor Colonel Weyn. Honor the correct-acting officers, Captain Indian and Captain Pumpernil. Honor the revolution, which protects you. This has been General Reilley speaking. Goodbye, then."

Frank spoke all that in kind of a fury and that's just about what he said, word for word, I don't think I could ever forget the sound of it. Ten dollars! I don't know why, but I had the feeling he was trying to buy something from me by saying that. He's crazy. That announcement would have stopped me from trusting Frank again if nothing else did, because if I know one thing, I surely know that Don never had Jerome Blackridge and George Meridel as "accomplices" in anything at all, and I was all the madder with Frank after he tried to get Don into still more trouble that way, so I called a special meeting of my propaganda committee.

We all got together in the propaganda headquarters, like before, but this time I just said, "How many of you are really sick and tired of this revolution?"

Nobody answered, not even Ham or Paul. Because they were scared. I could tell right away that they didn't trust me, they figured I was trying to find out if any of them had counterrevolutionary ideas, thinking I would report them to Frank.

I said, "I'm planning a counterrevolution."

This scared them even more than before.

Paul muttered, "Sure, and what about your loyalty oath?"

Sam Gabrenya said, "I'm not cruising for a revolutionary bruising, Colonel, sir, I'll tell you that."

I said, "I mean it! I mean it, and as for my loyalty oath, I'll just have to break it, that's all, and I don't care, because I'm an atheist and Frank should have never made me swear to anything on the Bible. I didn't want a loyalty oath in the first place, and I said so, but Frank just said we'd make a law against beatings like you got, Divordich, only he forgot to make laws against killing guys and framing guys and watching guys and threatening guys and scaring guys and making machines out of guys and teaching guys to fight dirty, and laws against telling lies of the kind that get people into serious trouble, and I just say that unless laws are absolutely perfect, so absolutely perfect nobody can get hurt because people, all people, are protected by the laws, then taking a loyalty oath is evil, that's what I say, it's evil." And I told them how Don Egriss had described his fight with Mason, and Gogo Burns said:

"Yeah, well maybe someone tossed that gun in there, maybe Blackridge did that, but it was still Egriss who shot that guy."

"Anyhow," Frank Divordich scratched various places on his face, "Frank arrested Blackridge and even put Meridel in The Brig for lying about you, so why are you complaining? Hell, you even got ten bucks out of it."

"I won't take any money from Frank," I said. Then I told them that my idea was that I was a colonel now, and I figured if I could just get rid of the one guy at the top, then I could take over the whole revolution, be General, and from then on I would just work to bring the whole revolution to an end, and I'd also make sure the revolution had some good ideals and make the guys really stand up for good things so long as it couldn't be stopped, if there was trouble about stopping it. I tried to speak with enthusiasm, like Frank does, and when I finished talking, I looked from face to face.

Nobody said anything. It was just about the longest silence in the world, we might as well have been all concentrating on the moon or sitting in a library or pretending we were posts in a fence or something. In a while I realized they weren't about to answer at all and I squinted around and decided they must have all been memorizing the Gettysburg Address just in case George Meridel got reinstated.

So I said, "Well?"

"Well what?" said Taylor Walk.

"Will you guys help me?"

More silence.

Ham said, "What if you get caught?"

I said, "Who cares? I've been in The Brig already and it was better than sitting in at the S.R.C., as long as Don is in The Brig, anyhow."

"How will you do it?" asked Ham.

"Well," I said, "there's nothing hard about it. The only hard thing is to get Frank to The Brig."

"Yeah?" Paul clacked his tongue. "What about Richardson? Rivaz? The girls? The Revolutionary Police?"

Well, I hadn't really thought everything out, as I told them, and maybe it was true we would need a few more guys with us.

Frank Divordich shook his head. "Not me, boy, count me out."

"You haven't got a chance," Paul mumbled.

"Anyhow," said Bob McCarthy, "who says it would be better having you for General? It's the revolution that stinks."

"Look," I told him, "I want to end it, don't I?"

"That's what General Reilley wants, too, according to him," said Sam Gabrenya.

"Hell, Win," said Ham, "how do you know the guys would obey you if you were General? You're pretty small."

198

That embarrassed me, so I said, "Because I'm a born leader, that's how I know."

Ham laughed but Paul said, "Ham's right. Frank has managed this whole thing since the beginning and if he went, then the whole revolution would probably just fall apart."

"Good!" I said.

That kept them quiet for a time, and we all suddenly saw how, if Frank was taken out of the revolution, the whole thing might end because there might be no one to hold it up. But the guys still wouldn't have anything to do with a counterrevolution, they were too afraid of being counterrevolutionaries, so at last I had to call the meeting to an end.

Paul said, "If anyone here says anything about what we've talked about, that guy will have to deal with the rest of us. Right?"

"That's right," said Bob McCarthy, "so no one better say anything."

"Yeah," said Ham, "my God, we have enough problems already."

I didn't say anything except to tell them the meeting was over and they could go do whatever they wanted, go swimming, smoke, go into the woods with girls— anything they wanted.

I just felt like being alone for a time, to think, but the only thing I could think of doing by myself would be to get that gun and make Frank go to The Brig. But I surely couldn't do that by myself, because he would take it away from me, knowing I would never shoot him. So there is nothing I can do.

Frank has planned a special party tomorrow afternoon for the smaller kids only, at the girls' mess hall. I think some of them haven't liked the parties with drinking and dancing and all, so that's why Frank had this

199

idea. He asked me what I thought about it, and I thought anything was a good idea to get away from the dancing and liquor parties which just make trouble, so I said it was a good idea. I had to write up announcements and members of my committee took turns making them. Only kids eleven years old and younger can go to that party, except some of the higher officers, and I may go myself, although Frank says he thinks he will have a special assignment for me tomorrow. I hope he doesn't, because I would kind of like to go to that party. Probably Irene will be there. I'm wondering what she is thinking of this revolution by now.

JUNE 19 AND JUNE 20

Last night I just couldn't write. I took out my diary and I opened it and I held my pen but I couldn't write, because now that Don Egriss is dead, I can hardly make myself care about anything.

It is terrible, and I am going to kill Frank Reilley. I wasn't there but there were a lot of rotten lies told about him and then they lynched him. It happened over at the girls' camp.

They said that Thelma Hogan now claims it was Don all along who had been the one to do that to her, and that Don had scared her so much she was afraid to report it; she said Don threatened he would "fix her" if she did. She says that she was scared of something happening and felt she had to report someone and since Don Egriss didn't like John Mason, Don had ordered her to report Mason. Then they had another girl, a smaller girl, announce that Don had threatened her, and they had this little girl make that announcement herself. I don't know what they must have done to make her say such a thing. Maybe they just convinced her that Don *did* threaten her. Frank could do that and he would, too, if he wanted to. Then they said Don had "bothered" other girls and what they finally did, of course, was to get all the girls over at Low Pines so furious that a whole big bunch of them just stood around the detention room over there, screaming and screeching at Don, and they got so mad that they said they wanted to give him over to the police right then. Frank was there to tell them they couldn't do such a thing. So they said that if Frank wasn't going to give Don to the police, they would lynch Don right on the spot, and Frank said that it wouldn't help for the girls to take the law into their own hands like that, and that however they looked at it Don had to have his trial, but they just said that Don never gave his "victims" a trial before he hurt them.

Then, suddenly, they went after Paul Indian, who was there and who is the one who told me all this, and about fifteen girls got around Paul and grabbed hold of him and he said he was so scared he nearly wet his pants, and the girls told Frank to let them have Don Egriss or they would take Paul instead, and right then, too. Paul was so scared he just shook and said he never knew how strong girls were when they got mad. He said he believed any one of them could have held him fast by herself, and he showed me his arms and neck where they held him, and their fingernails just dug at him so he was a whole lot of scratches and marks and loose skin and bloody places that will become scabs.

That's what happened and so Frank just let them take Don out of the detention room, and Paul says it was maybe fifty or even sixty girls just screaming like banshees who dragged Don off into the woods, and he might have been a baby the way they took him, and then Paul said you couldn't even see Don any more because of all those screaming girls around him, so Paul just sat down on the ground there and cried.

And those girls wouldn't let any boys come near until after, and then Don was just hanging from a tree with this rope around his neck, his head hanging crazy so that it made some boys sick just to see him there.

Paul said he was never going back to the girls' camp again.

Even before Paul finished telling me all these things, I fainted, but since I had fainted before up here, it didn't cause much interest. I was just taken to my cabin and put on my bunk and they put wet rags on my forehead until I woke up.

Paul also told me that the girls didn't even bury Don, they just cut him down from the tree and took him off in the woods somewhere, and they said they were going to let him make a stink for the worms.

I don't even know where he is.

Paul said that most of the girls were bigger girls but there were smaller girls, too, and Irene Mannering was one of those girls. I would like to hang Irene Mannering. I'd like to dig my fingernails into her skin and make her hurt and hit her and hang her. I hate girls.

After I woke up from fainting, Frank came to see me and I told him to go away, and I called him names but Frank said I was excited and mourning a friend and I should just rest all evening and I could make my report later, meaning the report I had been sent after in Wellberg, about how many high school and junior high school kids there are in Wellberg, and some other stuff. So Don is dead, and nearly everyone killed him, as far as I can see.

Frank told me this morning that they had to let the girls have Don, that too many kids in both camps wanted to either kill Don or turn him over to the police, anyhow, and there was danger of a counterrevolution just because of Don. And Paul Indian might have got killed if Don hadn't.

I didn't sleep at all last night. I just cried most of the night, I couldn't help it and I didn't even care who heard me.

This morning I had to go give that report to Frank about the kids in Wellberg, because Frank said yesterday that if we ever need a larger revolutionary force, we would have to try to recruit kids from Wellberg. So he sent me in with Manuel Rivaz to Wellberg and I had to stay there all day, because I was supposed to find out all sorts of crazy things, like in which districts were the places where the bigger kids got together, what they liked to do with their time, how happy or unhappy they seemed, really crazy things like that. I think Frank just wanted to get rid of me because he knew what was going to happen to Don. But I found out all that stuff, though I won't write about it here, and I had most of the report written out before I even got back to camp. So I just went over and gave it to Frank. I wouldn't trust him enough to have refused to give it to him. But I told him, when I gave him the report, that I wanted to quit as colonel, as adjutant, from the S.R.C., from everything.

Frank gazed at me a minute or so, twitching his eyes and looking both mad and sad somehow. "Because of Egriss?" he finally asked.

How Frank could be a straight-A student, I don't know. He's like a machine, like Thoreau said. He's crazy. I didn't even answer him. I just stood there hating him, and I couldn't help having tears in my eyes, and I still have tears in my eyes, and I think I will always have tears in my eyes from now on, and that is why I am writing this so messily, and I don't care.

But Frank said he knew Don was my friend but he didn't want me to resign just then, just when all this was making me so upset. Frank asked me, as a favor to him, to hold off quitting for a day or two, until I had time to see that it didn't much matter who killed Don

Egriss, someone was certainly going to, and it was better for the revolution, better for everybody, that we did it ourselves.

I didn't say anything. I just didn't want to stay with Frank any more. So I came back to my cabin. And then I found that book I gave Don on my bed, my Herodotus book, they had found it in Don's pocket, I was told later, and so it looked like he was a thief on top of everything else. I told guys how I gave that book to Don, but since everyone knew I liked Don, they just thought I was lying.

I hate everyone here except Paul and Ham. I hate everyone else. They are all sons of bitches and bastards and stinking scum and I hate them. I'm going to kill Frank Reilley, that is what I've decided. I will kill him myself and that will stop this rotten revolution. I will find a way to get that gun and then I will shoot him.

They didn't even call off the party for the little kids over at Low Pines. It just started late.

I will kill him, so now three guys will have been killed by this revolution, because I am going to kill his life out of him. Then they will have to kill me, so that will be four in all.

JUNE 21

All day Frank was in the Administration Building. I couldn't go in at all. He ate there and slept there and didn't come out even for a minute that I saw, almost like he knows what is in my mind and that I am just waiting for him to go away somewhere.

Someone told me today that the girls seem more resigned to the revolution after what happened to Don, and Evelyn Wright has made a number of announcements over there about *On Our Terms*.

I guess Frank is serious about getting recruits from Wellberg, because both yesterday and today he sent Manuel Rivaz into Wellberg. Yesterday Manuel went with Al Santangelo, who was promoted to Captain yesterday and is now on the S.R.C., but today Manuel went all by himself. I think Manuel has made some friends there and isn't coming back until late tonight, but I don't know what he is supposed to be doing, except that Manuel himself has been a little gloomy and he said something very mysterious to me: "Wellberg isn't the only place on the map." So I got the idea Frank might be sending Manuel to look at other nearby towns, too. What is Frank thinking? Is he actually trying to start a real revolution? I wanted to talk to Manuel Rivaz about trying to start a counterrevolution, but most of the guys just don't like to talk too much about serious things now, they don't even want to know about things which might be counterrevolutionary. So I didn't say anything to Manuel.

I was walking down by The Brig and Stanley Runk called me over to the window and he was real upset and he said, "Listen, Winnie Pooh, listen to me." He was so upset he was whispering and choking all at once. "I heard what happened to Egriss. Listen, kid, you got to believe me, see? I'm next. Reilley's going to get me next, he's got to get rid of me. Listen, Winnie Pooh, get me my knife. Get me that gun. Will you get me my knife? Just get me my knife, I'll make you General. You hear? I'll make you General. I'll go away, you can be General all by yourself. Listen, I'll give you money. What do you want? I'll give you anything you want, because you got to believe me, Reilley is going to get me next," and he was nearly crying and slobbering about it all, so I could see how he must have looked that time Jerome Blackridge took his knife away. "You got to help me, kid, you got to, you got to." I told Stanley that it would be all right, and I walked away. I didn't want to tell him I was going to kill Frank.

Mostly today, I just kept going back and forth from my cabin to the Administration Building. I didn't do anything at all. I've stopped looking at the mail, even hoping that some kid will write about the revolution, but I don't know if any of them really did, because I don't even care to read their letters.

Tomorrow maybe I will be able to go and see if I can find where they left Don, over around the girls' camp somewhere, but so far I haven't wanted to do this. But what I've decided to do is find him and leave my book with him, the Herodotus, since it was his—I gave it to him—and he even started to read it, because a corner of a page was bent over, at page 10, and I never bend corners.

Then I will go and see Howard, before I try to get that gun, in case anything goes wrong. I'll tell Howard where I hide my diary, so maybe they can understand why I want to kill Frank; Mama and my father and Uncle Giles I mean. I guess I'd better do that.

The whole camp is the same. The ground and the trees and the bushes and flowers and grass and even the weeds, all of them get together and make a big living smell that is delicious, and the river glides and slurps along as gently as always, and the birds get angry and get happy and peck about after food, and there are still trees full of pretty little black and white caterpillars, and there is always the moving sound of the slow wind which carries all these sounds and smells about, and the guys run around the trees and go into the river and swim and fart and horse around, they drill like drilling is a game which is fun, and the only thing more fun is lance practice, and the food is okay and you'd just think it was a normal summer camp, almost.

JUNE 22

Frank called a meeting of the S.R.C. real early, before breakfast, and said he was mad because Manuel Rivaz hadn't come back yet and that's how this day began.

Since no meeting could solve that problem, Frank said he wanted to put the platoons on special alert, in case anything is wrong, and so I was supposed to make some announcements about the possibility of another traitor. But after the meeting, I didn't even care to do it. I went and got my Herodotus book and then walked through the woods, clear over to the girls' camp, and I began to hunt for Don Egriss.

It was not hard to find where he was hanged, since Paul told me where it happened, straight up behind the Low Pines mess hall, and then I could see where they had cut him down, because part of the rope was still attached to the branch of that tree, and I wondered how those girls had got Don up so high, heavy as he was, but I guess they were just crazy and wild enough to do it.

I had to hunt a long time, it really was a long way and I went in many wrong directions and I was about to think I would never find him, and the thing that finally made me find him wasn't my eyes, but my nose, because he was stuffed into some wet bushes down by the water, beside a long stretch of the riverside where there are thousands of big and little rocks; it was a place where probably a lot of girls would never care to go swimming, since it would hurt their feet to walk on those rocks. And I suppose I wouldn't have seen him, except I smelled him, and so even though he smelled bad, about the same as that smell out where the caves are—which someone said must be full of dead rats—even so, I took him out of the bush, though it took all my strength and though I couldn't look at him for more than a couple of seconds. Something was happening to his body and his face and there were bugs on him, and he nearly didn't look like Don Egriss any more.

So I sat down and cried a long while, and then I put my Herodotus book on Don and I covered him over with a great lot of rocks. Then I built the rocks up higher and higher, so it would be some kind of monument, and then I got the idea to build them into the shape of a pyramid, which I thought Don would have enjoyed, because he was happy at the idea that the old Pharaohs had been colored.

It was miserable to leave Don there. I didn't know what to do after I finished the pyramid. There was nothing to do. So I went away.

I walked back through the woods to High Pines, and after sitting around the cabin a time I went up to the meadow where Howard's platoon was drilling and I told Howard I wanted to see him. He was just beginning to drill and said he was busy, so I told him I wanted to talk to him anyhow, and he said:

"Is that an order, Colonel?"

So I began to cry right there, in front of all those guys. Howard was furious. He went off with me and I thought he was going to beat me up or something, he was so mad, but then I told him I was going to kill Frank. Howard sat down on the ground and stared at me.

He said, "No you aren't."

I said, "I just wanted to tell you where my diary is."

"You aren't going to kill anyone! Just get the idea right out of your dumb little head!"

He was mad and so I just told him where I hide my diary, which is between two boards high up in the little lavatory behind our cabin.

Howard took my arm and squeezed it so hard I cried out and he said, "What a stinky place to hide anything, and you might as well not tell me, because I'm not going to get it. And you aren't going to kill anyone!"

So I came back to my cabin and Howard followed right after me and said he would kill me before he would let me kill anyone else, and he said he would beat me till I was broken in a hundred pieces, and he said he would tie me up and report me to Frank. He said everything he could think of saying, I guess, so I said, "All right, I won't do it." He didn't believe me, so he made me promise I wouldn't do it, and he made me promise that a number of times on my word of honor, and I did that because I wanted him to go away.

He only went away a little while ago, so I've taken my diary down and I've written all this, and after I finish I'll hide my diary again and then go and hang around the Administration Building, and for all I know I may never write in this diary again.

JUNE 22

Night.

The revolution is all over. Mr. Warren is dead, and I didn't get to kill Frank Reilley.

Manuel Rivaz came back late this afternoon, just before dinner, when everybody was gathering around the mess hall, and he had a whole army of policemen with him.

Nobody fought at all. The guards didn't stop them at the front of the camp, and they walked into the Administration Building and brought Frank out the same way as we did Mrs. Knute when the revolution began; and nobody fought at all.

Everyone was glad the cops came, except just a couple of guys, and Frank was mad as he could be, his eyes were twitching like crazy, or maybe he was only sad. Or scared. I don't know, but he was so excited he couldn't hold still while the cops were holding him.

I didn't know that Mr. Warren was dead until the whole revolution was over and the policemen couldn't find him. So Dick Richardson all at once broke up, he began to cry and he said, "Runk killed him, he's dead, it was Runk!" Then Richardson told how someone had telephoned Mr. Warren and Frank had brought him to the Administration Building. Frank told Mr. Warren to say only what he was told to say, and Stanley Runk stood by Mr. Warren with his knife just in case Mr.

Warren said anything wrong. Mr. Warren didn't say anything wrong, but after he hung up he began to argue with Frank and Stanley and called them hoodlums and so Stanley pushed him a little, and Mr. Warren lost his temper and slapped Stanley twice and Stanley kind of exploded and so they wrestled around a minute and Mr. Warren shoved Stanley down. Frank pulled Mr. Warren away, holding his arms back, and Stanley just leaped at Mr. Warren's stomach with his knife, and that is what happened. How awful!

So they put Mr. Warren away and cleaned things up and waited until everyone was asleep, and then Frank and Stanley and Dick Richardson all took Mr. Warren down, way down the river to the caves, leaving him there.

Everyone, especially the policemen, have been wondering what Frank's plans really were. They are wondering what he wanted with all that information from Wellberg and other places. They found some notes of Frank's about how both Low Pines and High Pines, the way they are set into the hills, can be defended by a fairly small group of people, and the notes were mainly maps Frank had drawn of the camps and meadows and woods and the river and the highway outside. It is hard to tell if Frank is just crazy, as he seems to be, or if he really did just lose control of things, and wonder if he could make this game into a real revolution which might accomplish something.

Anyhow, Frank doesn't say anything now, not to the cops and not to anyone else. He is nervous and mad and sad, and his purple eyes just kind of leer at things. He was that way when the cops came, and I guess he is probably that way right now.

After they had freed the counselors and cooks over at the girls' camp, they came over here and I saw

Edward Heinz looking around and so I said, "Hello, Mr. Heinz," and he went away. I guess I can't blame him for not liking me any more, seeing as how I was chairman of the propaganda committee.

They freed the guys at The Brig, Blackridge and Runk and Meridel, though they weren't letting Stanley walk around any, and I understand they freed some girls at the Low Pines detention room.

Soon they began to question us. I was questioned by a great big policeman who was fat and bald and he looked like he didn't like me at all, and I guess he really didn't, because he sounded like it, too. He said, "You were a colonel in this thing, is that right?"

"Yes," I answered.

"And you had a propaganda committee?"

"Yes."

"And you collected money from these kids to help this revolution, is that right?"

"Yes."

"Your name is Winston Weyn?"

"Yes."

"And he said real madly: "Yes, *sir!*"

"Yes, sir."

"Well, Winston Weyn," he said, "they tell me some real strange things about you. You know a kid named George Meridel?"

"Yes, sir."

"You put him in The Brig, so I guess maybe you do know him. Well, do you know what George Meridel says about you?"

"Yes, sir."

"Were you the kid who stirred up this whole revolution?"

"No, sir."

"A man and two kids are dead, they've been killed.

A pile of girls have got themselves hurt in a way they don't yet understand. That's what this revolution did. Was this revolution your idea, Winston Weyn?"

"No, sir." I began to feel a little like crying again, but I didn't really know if I could.

"You been reading stuff by a man named Karl Marx, haven't you?"

"I only have a book about political philosophers, sir."

"You have a whole pile of books, isn't that true?"

"Just a couple of books, sir."

"What does a kid your size want with a pile of books in the summer?"

"I just read them, sir."

"You've been doing quite a little bit of study about revolutions, haven't you?"

"I just read a few things about revolutions, sir."

"I'll tell you something I want you to deny, Winston Weyn. They tell me you don't like to say the Pledge of Allegiance. They tell me you don't like to sing *The Star Spangled Banner.* You want to deny that, don't you?"

"Just the last stanza of *The Star Spangled Banner,* sir."

"You mean you aren't going to deny what I just said?"

I thought about it and said, "No, sir."

He shook his head. "How old are you, kid?"

"Thirteen, sir."

"Thirteen is old enough to do a pile of damage, I guess. What do you think, Winston Weyn?"

"I guess so, sir."

So he stood up straight and peered down at me and shook his head some more and just began to turn away, but turned back to say, "Kid, you disgust me."

I said, "Yes, sir."

So he turned away and told another policeman, "Take this one, too."

By that, he meant I was to be one of the ones taken away in the police cars. There were about twenty of us at the boys' camp who had to be taken away, including Frank and Paul and Blackridge and Rivaz, even though he squealed, and others. But George Meridel didn't have to go. And Ham didn't have to go.

I am in a room with four iron beds in it, all of them as skinny as our bunks, and there are bars on the window, but all in all I guess it is nicer than The Brig, although the air smelled better up there. I am in a room with Manuel Rivaz and Dick Richardson and Al Santangelo. Manuel is just moody and lying very still on his bed, but Richardson and Santangelo have been arguing and don't seem to feel so bad as me and Manuel. Dick Richardson said that his cousin has a collection of butterflies and that he used to go and see them and they were very pretty, all mounted in little boxes and covered with glass, and it is a very difficult and interesting thing to do, collecting butterflies. But Al Santangelo says Richardson is nuts and that anyone who collects bugs has to be a bug himself. Of course, they aren't really mad at each other, they're only nervous and trying to pass the time away.

Tomorrow, Mama and my father will come here and I don't know if they will be able to get me out or not. But I know one thing, and that is that most of the policemen seem to think I am worse than anybody because I was chairman of the propaganda committee and took down the Bear Flag and didn't like the Pledge of Allegiance and things like that, and so, as I say, it doesn't seem like the revolution is over.

JUNE 23

I am writing just before dinner, which will be lamb chops, which I like very much. I am very lucky, I guess, because I am home again. It feels so good I can still feel it, even though I've been home since noon. Everything seemed brand new when I came home, and I felt so good about crazy things, like to sit on the couch or lie in the back yard, in the grass, and Mama has cooked everything I like best for lunch and dinner.

Even Howard is glad I came home and has treated me pretty well. The only thing is, it is my diary which got me home, and not Howard, or Mama or my father.

Of course, nearly everyone went home. In the end, the only guys they kept at the Juvenile Detention Hall were Frank Reilley, Stanley Runk, Jerome Blackridge and Dick Richardson, I think, who are all going to get examined by psychiatrists. And I think everyone else went home, even Manuel Rivaz, except I don't know about the girls, and I can't imagine what they will do to all those girls who did that to Don Egriss.

Most of us really got dressed down, I guess, and as I say, it was my diary which let me come home, because if I didn't have this diary, I just suppose I would still be in that Detention Hall with those four guys, that's how disgusted they were with me for the things I said and did. But they took my diary away this morning and went over it, and then I had to go and see a man who really dressed me down and told me I was wrong in just about everything I had done, who said I was too young to know what I was talking about, especially when it came to religion; but he said, almost like he regretted it, that he didn't think my intentions were so bad, but that "the road to hell is paved with good intentions," and he told me it wasn't bad to read and he could see that I was a "smart kid," but that I was still a kid and my reading should be guided by adults, and he meant to talk very seriously to my parents about this, and he was even going to look into my school to see who had been teaching me what. He said healthy reading would lead me to healthy thoughts, and that I should get out more and be more like other kids, and that healthy play leads to healthy growth, and I guess he is convinced I am sick, since he seemed mainly concerned about my health. And he said I was too young to understand how complicated social problems are, and that things are never just black or white, all good or all bad. He said he thought I am not a bad kid, and he would let me go home, but it was something like probation and I am supposed to be very careful about what I do for six months.

So I came home, and that was the best thing that happened today, nothing else seemed to matter, except that both my father and mother looked here and there in my diary and were hurt. I could see my father was hurt. He didn't get mad like I thought he would, but he was hurt all right, and just walked away without saying anything. I felt terrible. My mother cried after she looked into it. She just sat down and cried because of what I have written about religion, I guess.

But I can't help feeling happy about being home. I

feel guilty to be feeling happy, sort of, but I can't help it, because yesterday I would have said I could never be happy again. If only Don was alive and happy now, everything would be near perfect.

I know one thing, though. I will never go to another summer camp again. Never! I won't even go to a movie tomorrow, although Howard himself asked me if I cared to go (this is the first time he ever offered to let me go anywhere with him, but the crazy thing is, I don't care now like I would have before). I just want to stay home for a while.

JUNE 23

Night

Someone called tonight from the police and said they would want to borrow my diary as "evidence," so that decides the question about squealing: I won't have to squeal, my diary will squeal for me.

They called right after Uncle Giles came over, and when my father hung up and said what they wanted, Uncle Giles chuckled kind of an empty chuckle and said, "I told you that you'd be glad if you kept that diary up."

Then Uncle Giles came to my bedroom and sat on my bed and he read my whole diary through, I guess he read just about all of it and it took him a few hours, so I began to read *Bleak House,* which doesn't seem so bad, after all, once you get into it.

When he finished with my diary, Uncle Giles closed the book quietly, like it was the door to a library or something, and looked at me quite thoughtfully for some time.

All at once, he touched my knee and said, softly, "Colonel Winnie," and I could see he was sitting there liking me, while others had just been disgusted with me, and, well, I thought I just cried myself out of tears, but I had a few left, it seemed, and had to give them to Uncle Giles, crying I guess for Don and myself and the future that I'm now scared about, and just for something I couldn't understand, because everything is so changed now. I used to have this happy feeling about books and about knowledge, that there was nothing I couldn't learn, but now there are so many things I don't understand and don't know if I will ever be able to understand. So it seems I can't just study and figure out all the things I want to know, and that there are some problems people are supposed just to struggle with, just struggle with until the struggling itself works its way into some kind of answer. Just struggle.